I'll See You on Friday

I'll See You on Friday

Valerie Zahn

© 2022 by Valerie Zahn

All rights reserved. This book or any portion thereof may not be reproduced or used in any manner whatsoever without the express written permission of the publisher except for the use of brief quotations in a book review.

ISBN: 9798410326896 (paperback)

Chapter One

Abigail ran through the door of the hospital because of all the noise and commotion she heard going on in the streets. Roars, cheers, and shouts of joy were all around her. People were smiling, dancing, and celebrating. *"The war is over! The war is over!"* she kept hearing people say. She, like everyone else, was elated about the news. After all, she had spent the last three years as a nurse caring for the wounded soldiers. She had seen and heard about unimaginable things. With all the joy and excitement around her, a deep sadness filled her heart. She and her fiancé, Luke, had dreamed of this day, when the war would be over, and they could finally be married and spend the rest of their lives together. Even though this day had come, that day never would. Luke had been killed two years earlier in battle. She was determined that she would never find love again. Now the very thing that kept her busy and gave her purpose was over. *What am I to do now?* she thought.

She knew her grandmother would be thrilled to hear the news. She ran toward home to tell her. People were surprised to see Abigail on foot. Her family was one of the few in town that owned a car and had a chauffeur. Abigail was from an upper-class family. She lived in a very large home with her grandmother Lady Robinson and her servants. She didn't fit in with the other noble families, and it didn't bother her in the least. While other noble families looked down on those who were less fortunate, she befriended and spent most of her time with them. She was completely down to earth and treated everyone the same, regardless of their class or where they came from. As a result she was loved by those who lived in the village.

As soon as Abigail went through the front door, Murry was there to greet her. Murry was the butler. He had served her family since she was only a girl. He was a tall and slender man. His slicked-back hair had more gray now than red. "Have you heard the news, milady? After four long years, the war is finally over!"

"It is wonderful, Murry! Do you know where Grandmother is?" asked Abigail with a smile.

"She's in the study, milady, taking her tea. Can I get you some tea?"

"That would be wonderful. Thank you." Abigail walked into the study and found her grandmother reading the newspaper. "I see you've seen the news," said Abigail as she sat down.

"Did you know the queen is coming to our village next Friday? She's coming to give her condolences and express her gratitude to all the people who served and the families who lost someone," said Lady Robinson.

"Why isn't the king coming with her?"

"I'm not sure. The paper said he had to fulfill a previous engagement. It will be nice to see her in person again. I haven't seen her in years...well, since my wedding to your grandfather, before she became queen. I always knew she was destined for something great. I just didn't realize how great," said Lady Robinson with a shrug.

"Well, I don't plan on attending. There's nothing she can say to make me feel any better about losing Luke, and I just really don't want to go."

"You have to go, Abigail! It would be an insult to our queen. If nothing else, go for me."

Abigail sat there quietly, sipping her tea. She had so many different emotions stirring up inside her. Now with all her spare time, she would need to find something that would give her purpose. If she continued to live with her grandmother, she knew she had few options. For other girls her age, the sole purpose of living was to marry and have children. These weren't even considerations for Abigail.

A few days went by. There was so much hope and joy everywhere, even in the hospital. The number of patients was down. It was truly wonderful. Yet Abigail still felt a deep sadness and void. She knew she wasn't the only one. She knew all the mothers and widows of the fallen were feeling it too. She had visited many of them regularly after their losses. She decided to make some baked goods and visit them again. She knew the best way to get over something was to pour into others. She went to the local mercantile.

"Good day, Ms. Robinson. Can I help you find anything?" Mr. Henry wasn't accustomed to people of her class coming into his store, but Abigail was a regular. To him she was like everyone else.

"I don't need any assistance but thank you." She collected all the supplies she would need to make her baked goods, and she left.

When she got home, she went straight to the kitchen. Some of the servants helped her bring everything in. She found an apron and put it on. She washed her hands and was about to get started when Ms. Webb entered the kitchen. Ms. Webb was the family cook. She was a large woman with the sweetest smile. She made the most wonderful food. Other upper-class families had tried to get her to come work for them. She loved Lady Robinson and Abigail and would never consider leaving them. "Milady, would you like for me to make the food for you, or at least help?"

"I'm sure it would taste much better if you did, but you have enough to do just taking care of our meals. I will do it. Just do whatever you need to do, and don't let me get in your way," said Abigail as she put her arm around Ms. Webb.

"You could never be in my way, milady. I will be close by if you change your mind," said Ms. Webb as she picked up a pan to put it away. It took a few hours, but Abigail was able to make several pies and some different types of bread. Ms. Webb came into the kitchen. "It's time to change for dinner, milady."

Abigail rolled her eyes. "Formalities!"

"You did a wonderful job, milady. You are going to put me out of a job."

"Not a chance. Cooking is hard work." They both laughed. Abigail grabbed Ms. Webb's hands and looked into her big, tired green eyes. "Thank you for all of your hard work, Ms. Webb. I know we eat better than the king and queen."

"You are too good to me, milady," said Ms. Webb with tears in her eyes. "Now go get dressed for dinner before you get us both in trouble."

Abigail sighed and went upstairs.

The next day Abigail made her rounds and delivered the baked goods she had made for the different families. Her last delivery was to Mrs. Hickman. She was a widow who had lost her only son in the war three years earlier. When Mrs. Hickman saw Abigail at the door, her face lit up. "What a lovely surprise, milady."

Abigail reached out and handed her a pie.

"This looks delicious! You've been very good to me. I

could never repay you for all the kindness you've shown to me over the past few years."

Abigail smiled. "There is no need for repayment, Mrs. Hickman. I just wanted you to know that even though the war is over, your loss will never be forgotten. I will still be here for you however I can."

Mrs. Hickman, with tears running down her cheeks, reached out and hugged Abigail. They held each other and cried together. To lighten the mood, Mrs. Hickman pulled back, wiped her tears, and pulled out a folded-up piece from the newspaper from her pocket. "Did you hear about the queen coming here to our village this weekend, milady?"

"Yes! My grandmother told me," said Abigail. Abigail could see the excitement in her eyes, so she didn't want to show her lack of enthusiasm. Abigail felt the queen was a person like everyone else but had been gifted with a title. Although her feelings were different from everyone else, she didn't want to minimize the joy others had in her coming. "I must be going," Abigail said as she turned to walk away.

"Thank you again, milady. I hope to see you on Friday."

"You are most welcome, Mrs. Hickman. I hope so too."

The people in the village were very excited about the queen coming. Some of the men built a stage. Others tidied up the main streets and put large tents up. They decorated the streets and businesses with all sorts of beautiful flowers. The ones who could afford it purchased new clothing, all for making a good impression on the queen. Abigail thought it was all ridiculous, but she went along with it. She loved seeing the people of every class working generously together and looking forward to something. She joined right in. She put flowers all around the hospital. She helped all of the patients to look their best for the queen. The queen was arriving the next day, and she would be visiting the hospital.

Abigail woke up to Lillian, one of the servant girls, opening the curtains in her room to let the sunshine in. "Good morning, milady. It's Friday! The queen is coming today!"

"You make it sound like Christmas," responded Abigail sarcastically as she was stretching and getting out of bed.

"I've never seen her in person, only in the newspapers. Suppose she speaks to me! What should I say to her, milady?"

Abigail rolled her eyes. "She's a human being like anyone, so if she does speak to you, remember that and answer her like you would anyone else—except call her 'Your Majesty.'" They laughed.

"She'll be here in three hours. Where are you going to be when she's here?" asked Lillian.

"I will be with my patients at the hospital."

"So you're not going to be wearing one of your fancy dresses, milady?"

"No, I will be wearing my uniform, and I hope she never even notices me," said Abigail.

"I'll have your uniform pressed and ready here shortly, milady."

"Thank you, Lillian. I hope you have a wonderful time today."

"Thank you," said Lillian with excitement as she curtsied and left the room.

Queen Olivia arrived. The people were full of excitement. They waved and cheered. Her presence brought so much joy to the village. She shook hands and spoke with different people, expressing her appreciation and condolences for the many who had lost someone in the war. Queen Olivia looked in the crowd and saw a familiar face. She walked over to Lady Robinson. "Judith Robinson! It's been such a long time since I've seen you. How are you?" asked the queen.

"Splendid, Your Majesty," Lady Robinson responded as she curtsied in respect to the queen.

"I've heard the name Lady Abigail Robinson several times today by many individuals. They say she was a great encouragement to them during the war. Since you share the same last name, I was wondering if you are related?"

Lady Robinson smiled with pride. "Yes, she is my granddaughter."

"I would love to meet her. Is she nearby?" asked the queen as she searched the crowd with her eyes.

"She's a nurse, Your Majesty. You can find her at the hospital."

"Wonderful! The hospital will be my last stop. Can you introduce me?" asked the queen.

"Absolutely. I will meet you there," responded Lady Robinson. The queen kept making her rounds, greeting and talking with the people in the crowd. The press was there, taking many pictures of her at every turn.

A while later the queen entered the hospital. The patients and staff were elated to see her. Since it was a small hospital and the beds were laid out close together, the queen was able to stop and speak to each patient. Abigail wanted to stay out of the way, so she kept herself busy restocking and tending to the patients. Lady Robinson walked into the hospital, looking for Abigail. She couldn't see her in all the chaos. Then she saw her bending over, helping a patient with his drink. Just then the queen walked over to Lady Robinson, who curtsied when she saw her. "Your Majesty."

"So where is this infamous granddaughter I've heard so much about?" asked the queen in anticipation.

"She's over there, assisting a patient." Lady Robinson pointed toward Abigail.

"What a remarkable and beautiful young lady. Her parents must be extremely proud of her," said the queen.

"Her parents have passed, Your Majesty. Her mother died in childbirth, and her father, my son, died on March 28, 1914. A year later she lost her fiancé in the war."

The queen gasped. "Poor child! She's been through so much for someone so young, yet she serves and pours into others. I wish Prince Everett would settle down with such a young lady."

Abigail looked up and saw her grandmother, talking with the queen and motioning for her to come over to them. Abigail walked over and curtsied to the queen. "Your Majesty."

"I've heard such wonderful things about you today, Lady Abigail," said the queen.

"My grandmother only sees the good in me," responded Abigail.

"The wonderful things I heard about you didn't come from your grandmother but from your fellow villagers, which speaks volumes about you. Today your name was mentioned repeatedly by several different people. They kept saying what a gift you have been to the village, and they don't know what they would have done without you. I just wanted to say on behalf of the king and myself, thank you for serving Noreland with selfless kindness to your fellow man. You are a very special person," said the queen.

"Thank you, Your Majesty, for your kind words. But the truth is, these people gave me more than I could have ever given to them," responded Abigail.

"Just the kind of response I would have expected. I would like to invite you and your grandmother to join King John and me for a weekend at the palace. I will have to speak to the king and check our schedules, but I would love for him and Prince Everett to meet you, Abigail. I would love to catch up and talk about the old days with your grandmother as well."

Abigail hesitated. Lady Robinson interrupted, "We would be honored to come, Your Majesty. Thank you for the invitation."

"I look forward to it. I will let you know the actual dates soon," said Queen Olivia as she was leaving the hospital. Lady Robinson and Abigail curtsied. As soon as the queen left, Abigail glared at her grandmother. "What just happened?"

"We'll discuss it tonight at dinner," responded Lady Robinson.

Chapter Two

King John was sitting at the table, eating breakfast, when Queen Olivia came into the room. The servant pulled her chair out, and the queen sat down. She grabbed her napkin, placed it onto her lap, and the servant pushed in her chair. "How was your trip?" asked the king as he leaned over and kissed her on the cheek.

"I wanted to talk to you about it when you got back, but you were already in bed asleep when I came up." They both chuckled.

"I was beat! I had a wonderful time. The people were very kind and lovely. They made me proud to be their queen." A servant walked into the room, holding a platter with the newspaper on it. King John took it and began reading it aloud: "The queen dazzles her people with her beauty and kindness! The queen traveled all over Noreland to show her gratitude and express her condolences to the people. Her presence brought great joy and encouragement to everyone. She was gracious and kind and a true delight. Long live the king and queen!"

"It sounds like it went very well," said the king. With a look of disapproval, his eyes went down the page.

"What is it?" asked the queen.

"More scandalous news on Everett," he said as he folded the newspaper and threw it down onto the table. "We have to get that boy married."

"Oh, that reminds me. I met the most extraordinary young lady, truly a rare gem. She's the granddaughter of an old friend of mine from finishing school. I need you and Everett to check your schedules for next month and let me know when they can come for a few days. I really want the two of you to meet her," said the queen with excitement.

"I was thinking since we are a smaller country, we should find a princess and use a marriage to build an alliance with another country!" the king exclaimed. "I just want you and Everett to meet her. If he isn't interested, we can try other options."

Prince Everett walked into the room. He leaned over, kissed his mother, and sat down. "How did your trip go?"

"It went very well. You can read about it in the paper. It's the article above the one about you," said the queen with a disagreeable look in her eyes.

"You know those articles are mostly lies, Mother."

"The stuff they wrote about me seemed to be spot on, especially the beautiful part." The king and queen shared a smile.

"Look, Son, you're twenty-six years old. It's time for you to settle down and find a wife. You are going to be king one day. It's time you take things more seriously. If you can find someone with the right credentials, then you can choose for yourself. If not, your mother and I will choose for you."

Prince Everett looked down at his plate with frustration.

"In saying that, I need for you to look at your schedule for next month and give me some dates that you will have a few days open. I met the most remarkable young lady on my trip, and I want you and your father to meet her."

"I'm sure she's dull and unattractive, but she's beautiful on the inside, right, Mother?" responded the prince in a sarcastic tone.

"There's more to a young lady than her appearance, Everett," responded the queen sternly.

"You do want an heir, don't you?" exclaimed the prince. The king glared at his son with disapproval.

"I didn't get a good look at her because she was in a nurse's uniform, and her head was covered. But from what I saw, she seemed to be a very beautiful young lady from the inside and out." Everett rolled his eyes and continued to eat in silence.

Abigail and her grandmother were sitting at the table, having dinner. "Is Aunt Edna coming to visit anytime soon?" asked Abigail.

"Not that I'm aware of. Why do you ask, darling?"

"Things have slowed down a great deal at the hospital, and I feel like I could be of more use somewhere else. France suffered much worse than we did. Cousin Claudia wrote to me and said I could stay with her and Franco. I was thinking about going after the New Year celebration," said Abigail with hesitation in her voice.

"How long do you plan on staying there?" asked Lady Robinson.

"I'm not sure."

"This isn't about being useful, is it, Abigail?" asked Lady Robinson.

Abigail stopped eating and looked down at the engagement ring that she still continued to wear. "I suppose it's not." With tears welling up in her eyes, she said, "It's so hard to be here, Grandmother…with the war being over and things returning to some type of normal for everyone else when Luke isn't here. And he never will be."

"You need to start a new life, my darling, and find someone else. You're beautiful and smart. A man would be very lucky to get you—"

Abigail interrupted her grandmother. "I don't want another man. I'm like Papa. He never married after my mother died."

"Abigail, your papa had you. He felt by remarrying, it

would have made things harder for you. His attention and inheritance would be divided. It's not wrong to find love again. It doesn't make your love for Luke any less genuine. He would want you to be happy and to live your life to the fullest. You must ask yourself: What if you had been the one who died first? What would you want for Luke?"

Abigail responded reluctantly, "To be happy and to love again."

"All right, then. So try and find happiness. Find love again."

"I can't be happy with another man. I won't marry, Grandmother. He was the only one for me," said Abigail.

"Be that as it may, I hope you change your mind, but it's your life and your choice." She paused for a moment and continued. "I heard from the queen today. We are going to be visiting with them the weekend before Christmas. I can't wait to see the palace during the Christmas season! Aren't you excited, Abigail!"

Abigail looked at her grandmother sarcastically. "Do you even know me, Grandmother? I'm only going out of respect for the queen and to not embarrass you. This ordeal has nothing to do with me."

The servants looked at each other, smiling and trying not to laugh. Abigail finished her dinner in silence and then excused herself to her room.

Valerie Zahn

A few weeks later, Abigail and her grandmother were traveling to visit the king and queen. While Lady Robinson slept, Abigail looked out the window of the train, remembering her papa. Other than Luke, he was the only one who truly understood her. She wished she could talk to him and get some advice about what she should do with her life. He always knew exactly what to say. In spite of what her grandmother had said, she knew the real reason her papa hadn't remarried. It wasn't because of her but because he could not ever love another woman like he had loved her mother. The way he talked about her made Abigail feel as though she actually knew her mother. They had a rare type of love that even death couldn't stifle.

She remembered her many train rides and adventures with her papa, visiting new places and meeting new people. He was a very intelligent man who knew and understood how to do many things. He would travel to help people sort out their books and finances. He enjoyed helping people however he could, and people called on him often. He was the one who had encouraged her to be a nurse while others frowned at the idea. After all, she was of the upper class; she wasn't supposed to lift a finger. Her papa encouraged Abigail as a young girl to play in the mud and get her hands dirty. But he also made sure she had the proper training to survive in the upper-class world. It was from her papa that she learned a true knowledge of God. He taught her, through example, to love everyone in spite of all things and to serve others. To put others above herself. He would take her to hospitals and visit the sick. He would bring the patients sweets and candies to lift their spirits. Before he would leave, he always said a prayer over them if they allowed it.

Abigail remembered one extremely cold night as a girl when she and her papa were getting off a train. They walked by a homeless man with basically nothing to his name. He was sitting on the ground, shivering, and he never asked for anything. Her papa took off his expensive coat and gave it to the man. He helped him up and took him to the nearest motel and paid for him to have a hot meal and a place to stay for the night. She had never met anyone who genuinely loved people the way he did. She felt very grateful for a papa who would teach her these treasures.

With tears in her eyes, she remembered her last conversation with him as he fought for breath. She was sitting beside him on his bed, holding his hand. He said, "I am so very proud of you, my darling, and the woman that you have become and the woman you are becoming. Your mother would be just as proud. You remind me so much of her. Always remember the words of Jesus: 'To love the Lord with all your heart, with all your soul and with all your strength, and to love your neighbor as yourself.' God has given you a healthy mind and body. He's given you wealth. Use it all for Him. I love you, my darling, and love never dies." He put his other hand over hers, closed his eyes, and breathed his last. Since that day she had tried her hardest to follow his instructions. She intended to spend her entire life in service to God by loving others. She didn't know what that would look like, but she knew God would lead her and guide her as He always had.

Chapter Three

When Abigail and Lady Robinson got off the train, a chauffeur was there to meet them. He drove them to the palace. On their way there, they enjoyed the scenery. Lady Robinson pointed out some of the historical places. She was very excited. Abigail had visited them before with her papa. She had never seen her grandmother so giddy. Abigail just wanted to get it over with. She was determined to hold back her true feelings and go with the flow. She was tired of formalities and crowd pleasing. She loved her king and queen and genuinely respected them; she just felt very out of place.

When they arrived, a tall man in his mid-twenties with blond hair was standing outside the private doors of the palace to greet them. As soon as they got out of the car, he came over and introduced himself. "My name is Archie. I will be here to assist you in any way that I can to ensure that you have a wonderful time during your stay at the palace. The king and queen are anxious to see you. They would have been here to greet you, but they had another engagement that they simply could not miss. They are, however, looking forward to seeing you tonight at dinner, which is at seven p.m."

Some of the servants took their bags and carried them in. "Please come with me," said Archie as he walked ahead. They followed him into the palace and just stood there, admiring what was before them.

They had never seen anything like it. It seemed surreal that they were actually standing inside the palace. The palace represented the monarchy of their history, which they had learned about when they were children. "I thought our home was large," said Abigail with a laugh.

"It is quite something. I will be giving you a tour of the palace tomorrow. For now you should get settled in and rest before dinner. Is there anything you need from me before I go?" asked Archie.

"No, that will be all," responded Abigail.

"Very well, miladies. This is Nina and Kate. They are the maids who will be taking care of you for the next couple of days." The girls curtsied. "Follow them, and they will show you to your rooms."

They walked up a very large staircase with many stairs, which was a little difficult for Lady Robinson. Abigail stood beside her and held out her arm to help her up the rest of the way. They each had their own suite with a bed and sitting area.

The maids helped the ladies get settled in and said they would return at six p.m. to help them get changed for dinner.

Lady Robinson was tired from the trip and wanted to lie down and rest. Abigail was tired of sitting and wanted to tour the palace gardens but didn't want to inconvenience anyone. She knew she couldn't walk around the palace without supervision, so she settled for reading a book. After all, she only had an hour before the maid would be back to help her change.

Abigail held onto her grandmother as they walked down the stairs. The king and queen were waiting for them at the bottom of the staircase to welcome them before they went in for dinner. "She's even more beautiful than I remembered," said the queen with delight.

"I don't see how Everett can find anything wrong with her—well, other than the fact that you chose her," said the king with a grin.

"Where is he? He's supposed to be here," remarked the queen with frustration.

When Abigail and Lady Robinson reached the bottom of the stairs, they both curtsied. "Your Majesties."

"How was your trip, ladies?" inquired the queen.

"Splendid. Thank you for inviting us. We are honored to be here," said Lady Robinson.

"We are glad you could come. I've heard a lot about you, Lady Abigail," said the king. Abigail looked at her grandmother.

"It wasn't from your grandmother; it was from me. When I visited your village, the people simply raved about you. I wanted the king and Prince Everett to meet you. Speaking of Prince Everett, he's supposed to be here. I'm not sure what is keeping him. I suppose we will wait a few more minutes. Maybe he will join us soon," said the queen.

Just then a servant came over, bowed, and handed her a note. She read it and sighed with aggravation. She handed the note to the king, who gave a similar reaction. "I guess he won't be joining us tonight after all. He will, however, be giving you a tour of the city tomorrow morning around ten o'clock if that's all right with you, Lady Abigail?"

"That would be lovely," she responded, hiding her true feelings. It wasn't like she could say no to her queen.

"Wonderful. That's settled. Shall we go in for dinner?"

They all followed the king into the dining room. It was very traditional, with a large chandelier and a beautiful centerpiece in the middle of the table. Everything was so big and grand. It all seemed surreal to Abigail that she and her grandmother were actually dining with the king and queen. Abigail remained poised, never showing her nerves or discomfort. The king and queen were very impressed with her. The king tried to find a flaw in her and wasn't able to. "I wanted to say thank you for your service to our country by serving as a nurse during the war and helping our wounded."

"It was my pleasure, Your Majesty. I only wish I could have done more."

"I heard that you lost your fiancé in the war; he was a brave young man. It's men like him that make our country so great," said the king.

Abigail paused and collected herself. "I agree, Your Majesty. He was very brave. I'm thankful to have known him."

"Are you currently courting or interested in anyone?" inquired the queen.

"No, Your Majesty. I've not even been looking," responded Abigail.

"A girl as beautiful and kind as you has plenty of options to choose from. I believe Prince Everett is available at the moment. He hasn't introduced us to anyone if he's not," said the queen.

Abigail was thankful when the queen changed the subject and began reminiscing with her grandmother. Abigail quickly realized this trip was more about a possible love match between her and the prince rather than old friends catching up. Since he had not shown up for dinner, it was obvious that he felt the same way about it as she did. She felt very embarrassed. She wished she could just hide in her room for the next few days. How was she to face him tomorrow? She was hopeful that he wouldn't show up then either.

The next morning Prince Everett was standing with Archie at the bottom of the staircase, waiting for Abigail. "After she comes down, I will introduce myself and apologize, saying that something has come up. You then will fill in for me and occupy her for the rest of the day," said the prince. They both looked up. Abigail was coming down the stairs.

She was wearing a light blue dress that complemented her big blue eyes. Her dark hair was pulled back under a white hat. "Is that Lady Abigail?" asked the prince.

"It is, Your Highness."

"Are you sure it's the same lady Her Majesty is urging me to meet?" The prince was in total shock that his mother had picked out someone so beautiful. She usually chose women for him who had "inner beauty," as she called it, but were not so easy on the eyes. He never took his eyes off her as she was walking down the stairs. "Disregard everything I said before. For the first time, I will appease my mother."

As Abigail was coming down the stairs, she noticed that the prince was even more handsome in person than in the newspapers. She wouldn't allow herself to look into his dark-brown eyes. No wonder women threw themselves at him. *Not this woman*, she thought. It took more than looks to woo her, and besides, her heart had already been given to another.

When Abigail reached the bottom of the stairs, she curtsied. "Your Highness."

"You must be Lady Abigail. I've heard so much about you. Are you ready for me to show you around?"

Abigail hesitated. "Before things go any further, I wanted to apologize to you about this visit. I genuinely thought the reason for our invitation was for my grandmother and Her Majesty to reconnect. After dinner last night, I realized it was really about us meeting and maybe a possible love connection, which is something neither of us want. If I had known this before, I never would have come. Please know that I'm genuinely sorry. I don't want to waste any more of your time. I'm sure you have other things to do. Perhaps Archie can show me around."

The prince stood there in shock. He had never had a woman talk to him that way before. She talked to him as if he were just a man and not the prince. This made him very intrigued with her. "Please don't apologize. If anything, I'm the one who needs to apologize to you. I'm sorry they put you through that. I wish they would stop trying to marry me off and let me find someone on my own. It would be my pleasure to show you around. After all, I wouldn't want to upset Her Majesty any more than she already is after I missed dinner last night."

"If you insist, and I'm really not imposing. I would love to see the palace gardens," said Abigail with a smile.

"Are you sure you don't want to see the city instead?" asked the prince.

"I'm sure. If we go out in public, our pictures are going to be plastered all over the newspaper, and I rather like my privacy."

He was taken aback by her response. Every woman he had ever met wanted her picture in the newspaper. "You do make a good point. I like my privacy also, but I don't get much of it. Shall we?" asked the prince as he held out his arm for her to hold onto.

They walked out to the palace garden. Abigail's face lit up. "It's so beautiful. Is it ever hard for you to believe this is your backyard?"

"I guess I never really thought of it like that. If you think this is beautiful, you should see it during the other seasons," responded the prince. As they walked through the garden, Abigail tried to take it all in. She loved being outside in the fresh air and the smell of the flowers. "I heard you were a nurse during the war. Let me just say thank you for your service to our country."

"Thank you for your kind words, but they are unnecessary. I wish I could have done more—"

"More?" he interrupted.

"I would have fought if they would have let me."

They both laughed. "I've never heard a lady say such a thing," responded the prince.

"I say a great many things you wouldn't expect to hear from a lady." Realizing what she had said, Abigail laughed. "Not things unladylike. What I'm trying to say is, even though I am considered upper class, I find it dull and a waste of life. Most upper-class girls my age feel their entire life revolves around getting married. After they get married, they spend the rest of their days throwing or attending balls, entertaining, crowd pleasing, and gossiping about their own kind. I feel that life should be about more than all that. I believe we should use what God has given us and contribute to the world by being useful and helping the less fortunate."

"So how do you plan on fulfilling your purpose and contributing to the world?" asked the prince in amusement.

"Well, after the New Year celebration, I plan to travel to

France and help out there for a while. And after that, I'm not sure, but I know something will come up. I suppose I'll go wherever I can be useful."

"So do you ever plan on finding love and marrying?" asked the prince.

"I have experienced true love. I was engaged." She looked down at the engagement ring. "He was killed three years ago in the war. I never plan to give my heart to another man." She paused for a second, trying to change the subject. "Enough about me. Are the things they write about you in the newspapers true?"

"Some of it but not most of it. I do enjoy the company of a beautiful lady, and occasionally I have a drink or two, but I'm not the wild, immature, spoiled prince they portray me to be. I suppose it sells papers. It's because of the things they write that the king and queen want me to settle down and marry. I'm just not ready for that, and I may not ever be. If I do marry, I want it to be with someone that I love, someone I've chosen. I don't want the mediocre love most people have. It's not easy having your life always planned out for you and having little to no say about it. I often feel like I'm in a fishbowl. I feel trapped and have eyes on me constantly watching. I often wish I had the freedom you speak of. I also have the pleasure of knowing that someday I will be king and the great responsibility that it brings."

Abigail could see the honesty in his eyes. She stopped walking and turned toward the prince. "I'm so sorry for the burden you carry. Thank you for sharing what troubles you and for drawing my attention to my own selfishness and not even realizing that a prince has struggles too. If there is anything I can ever do for you, don't hesitate to ask."

The prince was caught off guard. Was she pitying him? He had never intended to share this; it had just come out. He could see her compassion and sincerity in her eyes. He saw the inner beauty his mother had often spoken of. Even though her outer beauty was exceptional, her inner beauty far surpassed it.

They finished their walk in silence. "Well, this concludes our tour. Thank you for accompanying me and also for the interesting conversation," said the prince.

"Thank you, Your Highness, for a wonderful day. I'll never forget it. Please don't worry about coming to dinner tonight; there is no obligation."

"Not from you, maybe, but there is with the king and queen."

"I will tell them that I told you not to come. The blame will fall entirely on me. Besides, I'll most likely never speak to them again after tomorrow. It's all right if they don't like me. And if I don't see you before I leave, it was nice to meet you. You are not at all what I expected," Abigail said with a sweet smile.

The prince reached down, grabbed Abigail's hand, and kissed it. "No, Lady Abigail, the pleasure was all mine." She curtsied, and they went their separate ways.

At seven p.m. sharp, Abigail and Lady Robinson were downstairs with the king and queen, ready to go into the dining room. "How was your day with the prince, Abigail? Did he show you around the city?" asked the queen.

"It was a lovely day. I had a wonderful time. He was planning on showing me the city, but I asked to see the palace gardens instead of going out and drawing attention."

The queen tilted her head in surprise. "I've never heard a lady say she didn't want to draw attention."

"As you know, Mother, she is no ordinary lady," said the prince as he was walking into the room. He stood next to Abigail, who was surprised to see him.

"I didn't think you were joining us for dinner," said Abigail with a confused look on her face.

The queen leaned over to the king and whispered, "I guess it did go well today."

The prince pulled Abigail away from everyone else. "Were you being genuine when you said if there was anything you could do for me to ask?"

"Absolutely," said Abigail.

"Can we talk alone after dinner? I think I have figured out a solution that will help both of us."

Abigail was anxious to hear his proposition. What could it possibly be? Just then the butler invited everyone into the dining room for dinner. Abigail was quiet throughout dinner, trying to figure out how she could possibly help the prince. Lady Robinson and the queen went on and on about their day and shared stories of when they were girls, stories Abigail had heard dozens of times.

After dinner, the prince stood up, pulled back Abigail's chair, and took her hand. "Please excuse us. We need to discuss something."

"Take your time," said the queen with excitement in her voice. She and the king glanced at each other and smiled.

The prince took Abigail to the study and closed the door for privacy. "Since our conversation earlier today, I've been thinking. My parents want me to be married by my twenty-seventh birthday. That's in five months. If I haven't chosen anyone to marry, they are going to choose one for me. If the king has his way, I will have to marry some spoiled princess from God only knows where and possibly live a miserable, loveless life. You have said that you will never give your heart to another man. You have no expectation of loving again. My proposition is: What if we marry only legally? This will appease the king and queen and prolong things for me to be able to find true love."

Abigail sat down in a chair, perplexed at this literal proposal. "Did I just hear you right? You are wanting us to be married to give you more time to find a wife?" She was very confused. "Suppose you do find love? You are to be the head of the church. You can't just get a divorce to marry someone else," said Abigail.

"True, but if we never consummate the marriage, then the marriage can be annulled, and things can carry on as if we never wed. I'm aware of the scandal it will cause. However, it would be less of a scandal than a possible divorce."

Abigail sat there thinking it over as the prince continued. "This will be beneficial to you by allowing you to serve people on a much larger scale. You'll have more doors opened for you because of your title, and you will always have my support in all you choose to do."

Abigail didn't say anything at first.

"I know this is a lot to ask, and if you don't want to do it, I will completely understand."

"You are willing to go through all of this for the sake of finding true love?" asked Abigail.

"Absolutely! Don't you understand? I don't have the luxury of choosing my career, where I get to live, or a life of privacy. In almost every part of my life, I have so little say. I at least want to be able to choose the woman I get to spend the rest of my life with," said the prince with hopelessness in his voice.

"Let me pray and think this over tonight. I will give you an answer before we leave in the morning."

The prince smiled in relief at the thought that she was even willing to think about it. They left the study, and Abigail went back to her room instead of joining everyone else in the drawing room for cocktails.

Abigail paced the floor all night, praying and thinking it all over. It was one of the longest nights of her life. She wished she could hear God's voice audibly shouting out what she should do.

It never came. She tried opening her Bible, hoping the answer would pop out at her. It never did. It now came down to faith. She remembered the verse that said His sheep know His voice. She sat there on her knees in silence, waiting and listening. It finally came to her, and she knew what she needed to do.

At dawn she packed up and had breakfast in her room. There was a knock on the door. She opened it. It was her grandmother. "I'm going down for breakfast. I was wondering if you would like to join me."

"I've already eaten," responded Abigail.

"You never eat your breakfast that early. Are you all right, darling? You look exhausted. Did you not sleep well?"

"I'm fine, Grandmother. I will come down after breakfast." Lady Robinson went on her way. She knew something was bothering Abigail, but she knew now wasn't the time to find out. A little while later, the servants brought down the luggage. Abigail walked down the stairs to join her grandmother. The king and queen were at the bottom of the stairs, as well as Prince Everett, who was eagerly waiting to hear Abigail's answer. When she reached the bottom, Abigail curtsied. "Your Majesties. Your Highness."

"We missed you at breakfast. Are you feeling all right?" asked the queen with concern.

"I'm well, Your Majesty. Thank you for asking. I was just hungry a little earlier than usual," Abigail said with a laugh.

"Thank you for having us. We had such a wonderful time," said Lady Robinson.

"We did as well. Perhaps we can do it again sometime," said the queen. She looked at the prince, who was looking at Abigail.

"We would like that," responded Lady Robinson.

Abigail looked over at Everett. "May I have a word with Your Highness in private?"

He took her hand in haste and led her into the study. He closed the door with urgency. She stood there for a second. "I didn't sleep a wink. Are you sure about all of this?" she asked with uncertainty.

"Completely!" responded the prince as he waited in anticipation for her answer.

"If you agree to my terms, then I will do it."

Confused, he asked, "So what are your terms?"

"First off, God is number one to me, not the king or queen, you or the country. Don't ever try to change me. I will never try and change you either. We accept each other as we are. Second, never lie to me. Always tell me the truth, even if you know it's going to hurt or make me angry. Lastly every Friday we have a date night. It obviously won't be an actual date but time we set aside every week for us to be friends. This way we can be on the same page and have an idea of what's going on with each other so that when we are in interviews or others ask, we aren't complete strangers and can give honest answers about each other."

The prince sat there for a moment. He stuck out his hand. "Agreed!" They shook hands.

"With all that being said, will you marry me?" asked the prince.

She laughed. "Let's hope your next proposal is much more romantic."

"I'll work on it." They both laughed.

"I will. So what happens now?" asked Abigail.

"As soon as possible, you will need to remove your engagement ring from your finger." Abigail looked down at her ring, holding back tears. "Perhaps you can wear it on a necklace around your neck so that it can be close to your heart," said the prince with compassion. He genuinely felt bad about asking her to do this but knew it needed to be done. "Next, when you leave here today, you will need to get your affairs in order and be back here in a month to start etiquette lessons, get a new engagement ring, and begin planning for the wedding." She stood there, trying not to show her nerves. He reached down and grabbed her hand. "Let's go and tell our families the good news. Her Majesty will be so happy she may dance a jig." They laughed as they walked out of the study, holding hands.

The king, queen, and Lady Robinson all looked at each other.

"We have an announcement to make. We plan to marry," said the prince.

"Congratulations!" said the king and queen unanimously. All formalities were forgotten, and everyone began hugging one another.

After all the excitement, Lady Robinson exclaimed, "We best be on our way. We don't want to miss our train."

"We will see you here in a month to begin etiquette training and planning the wedding. I'm so excited!" said the queen with delight. "You're welcome to come with her, Lady Robinson. We are family now."

The chauffeur stepped in. "We must be going, miladies, or you will miss your train."

Prince Everett leaned over and whispered in Abigail's ear, "Thank you for doing this for me." He took her hand and kissed it.

The two ladies were on their way. Lady Robinson was giddier on the way home than she had been on their way there. Abigail was having a hard time processing all that had transpired over a short period of time and how drastically her life was about to change.

"Now I want all the details, from the moment you met the prince until the moment he proposed. I never saw this coming," said Lady Robinson.

"I will tell you, Grandmother. It's not the romantic fairy tale you think it is, but I suppose it's an interesting story," responded Abigail with a smile.

Chapter Four

The servants were very excited about the arrival of Lady Robinson and Lady Abigail. They especially loved Lady Abigail. She always made them feel valued and appreciated. They had really missed her, even though she had been gone for only a few days. Mr. Murray and many of the other servants were standing out to greet them. "How was your visit, miladies?" asked Murry.

"Oh, we have much to tell. Call all the servants together at once. We would like to tell everyone at the same time," said Lady Robinson with a huge smile on her face.

Mr. Murry was very curious to hear the news. In his twenty-two years of serving the family, he had never seen Lady Robinson so happy. She looked as though she were going to burst with excitement. Lady Abigail didn't seem excited at all—quite the opposite. Mr. Murry gathered all the servants together in the drawing room. The servants were very puzzled and confused. *What could this possibly be about?* they wondered. They chattered among themselves. Lady Robinson and Lady Abigail entered the room, and everyone went quiet. "I know it is quite strange to call you all together like this, but I wanted to tell everyone together. The news you are about to hear is completely confidential. It will not be officially announced for another month. If word gets out, I will know exactly where it came from." She paused for a moment to hold out the suspense. "The news is...Lady Abigail is engaged to Prince Everett!"

Everyone gasped in shock. Then, there were roaring cheers and congratulations. Abigail loved seeing the staff so happy and joyful. She wished she were as excited about it as they were. She felt a bit of grief and sadness. Her entire life was about to change forever. She would never be able to go anywhere in her country without everyone knowing who she was. This was a huge sacrifice, but she was willing to do it for her future king.

When Abigail woke up the next morning, the same feelings of sadness lay in the pit of her stomach. She decided for the next month she was going to do all the things that were "normal" for her. She was going to savor every moment. Today she decided to go to work at the hospital. She didn't know if they would let her volunteer her services as a nurse once she became a princess. She was at least going to try. Since the war was over, there wasn't as much need for nurses. She told her chauffeur that she wanted to walk today and probably most days for her last month at home. She knew walking longer distances in public would never be an option for a princess. Even though it was cold out, she wanted to take in everything and enjoy it all. She loved the village and the people there. She knew the people there loved her too. She hoped that would never change.

Every direction she looked was filled with memories—memories of being a girl and memories of her papa and Luke. Some memories were wonderful; others were not. All of them were a part of her and contributed to the woman she was, and she was grateful for them all.

While walking through the churchyard, she looked over at the large old pine tree that seemed to have been there as long as she could remember. She remembered a beautiful Sunday afternoon. Everyone had left after church but Luke and her. They sat under the tree, talking. He had looked into her eyes and kissed her for the first time.

She stopped and stood there for a while. Holding back the tears, she kept walking. As she was walking, almost everyone she met smiled and greeted her by name. She stopped and talked to a few of them. She realized she had taken for granted the friendliness and genuineness of the village folk. She never would again. Even though she had planned to leave for France for a while, she had planned to return and hoped things would go back to normal. After marrying the prince, even after the annulment, she knew people would never treat her the same.

She remembered the scripture in the Bible that said, "Greater love hath no man than this, that a man lay down his life for his friends." Although she knew she wasn't literally laying her life down, she felt like she was in a sense.

Prince Everett was fly-fishing with his best friend, Lord Macentire—or, to him, Andrew. They had been best friends for as long as he could remember. They were more like brothers than friends. Although they had many similarities, they were also quite different. Andrew liked to be the center of attention, which at times could be frustrating to him, as Prince Everett received more attention because of who he was. Andrew was also very charismatic and flirtatious and was the life of every party. The prince wished on many occasions that their roles could be switched around, that Andrew could be the prince.

"Do you have anything on your schedule for April fourth? If you do, I need you to reschedule because I need you for something," said the prince.

"I don't know of anything right off. What do you need me for?"

"I need you to be my best man at my wedding."

Andrew dropped his pole. "What! Are you joking?" Andrew searched Prince Everett's face to see if he was telling the truth. "Whom are you marrying? I didn't know you were seeing anyone, let alone in love."

"Who says you have to be in love to marry? After all, I am a royal."

"Oh, so the king and queen have forced you to marry?"

"She was someone my mother liked and introduced me to, but it was entirely my decision to ask her."

"So let me get this straight. You weren't forced. And you don't love her. And you asked her to marry you? What am I missing?"

"We get along well. We understand each other. We both feel trapped in our lives, so we have an arrangement that will help us both."

"I really don't understand what you're saying," said Andrew as he cast his line back into the water.

"I have to be wed by my next birthday. However, if we don't consummate the marriage and I find love, we can have the marriage annulled, and everyone lives happily ever after."

Andrew dropped his pole again. "And she's actually willing to do this?"

"Surprisingly yes."

"It must be her lifelong dream to become a princess or to be in the spotlight."

"No, she rather hates attention. I offered to take her out and show her the city, and she wanted to stay at the palace and walk the gardens instead. She said she didn't want to draw attention or to have her picture in the newspapers," responded the prince.

"There must be an ulterior motive. You're never going to get out of this. What have you done?"

"She's not like anyone you've ever met, Andrew. You just have to meet her before you make judgments about her. She's not like anyone I've ever met either. She's beautiful, kind, genuine—"

Andrew interrupted, "Are you sure you're not in love with her?"

The prince rolled his eyes.

"So when can I meet this girl?"

"Her name is Abigail. She's coming back here in a month for etiquette training and wedding planning."

Andrew cast his line in the water again. "All I'm going to say is enjoy your last month of freedom."

"It's not like that. Out of the entire week, I only have to give her a few hours of my time every Friday."

"Every Friday! That's when most of the best social events are! Like I said, enjoy your freedom while you still can," said Andrew with a sarcastic smile.

Abigail only had one week left. Where had the time gone? She had pushed this off for weeks, and now she knew she had to do it. She walked up the stairs to the modest home. Luke didn't come from a family that had money. It was one of the qualities she loved best about him. Before she knocked on the door, she stood on the porch, reminiscing about all the conversations and dreaming of the future that had taken place there. Holding back tears, she knocked on the door. She tried to prepare herself that Luke wouldn't be the one to answer the door. He wouldn't be in the living room with a smile on his face greeting her with a kiss. The door opened. It was Luke's mother, Deborah.

"Abigail! What a wonderful surprise!" She reached out and hugged Abigail. No preparation could subside the ache in her heart for the absence of Luke. She began to cry. "What's wrong, sweetheart?" asked Deborah as she held her in her arms.

Abigail couldn't say anything at first. The tears wouldn't stop.

"I know it's very hard for you to be here." Deborah continued to hold Abigail and to cry with her. Luke's father walked in. He put his arms around both women.

After a few minutes, Abigail pulled herself together. "I have to tell you both something, and I wanted you to hear it from me first before you hear it from someone else."

"What is it? Are you alright?" asked Deborah with concern.

"I'm fine. There's nothing wrong." She hesitated. "I'm... getting married. I'm marrying Prince Everett."

Luke's parents looked at each other and sat down in shock. "The prince?" they asked together.

"I wanted you to know that I'm not marrying for love. My heart still and always will belong to Luke, and I have shared this with the prince. I'm marrying to help the prince with a dilemma. He's being forced to marry before his next birthday, and he chose me," said Abigail with sarcasm in her voice.

"What about you, Abigail? How do you feel about this?" asked William, Luke's papa.

"It will give me a larger platform to serve others."

Deborah could see how hard the decision was for her. She placed her hand over Abigail's. "You owe us no explanation. We know how much you loved Luke and how much he loved you. He would want you to move on. If one day you develop feelings for the prince, it is all right. Luke would want you to be happy, and so do we."

"That's not going to happen," said Abigail abruptly."

"Maybe not, but if it does, don't feel guilty. And know you will always have our blessing. Our greatest desire for you is to be happy." Deborah got up, walked into the kitchen, and made them all tea. Abigail visited with them for a while. They cried and laughed, telling stories from the past and remembering Luke.

Lillian, one of the servant girls, ran downstairs to tell the good news to Ms. Webb, the cook; she was like a mother to her. Ms. Webb was chopping carrots and preparing dinner. Lillian was so excited she could barely speak. "Spit it out, child. I haven't got all day," said Ms. Webb with impatience.

"Ms. Webb, Lady Abigail has asked me to come with her

to the palace to be her maid. Can you believe it? She chose me!"

"I'm very happy for you, child. You are a hard worker. You deserve this," said Ms. Webb with a tender smile.

"Oh, I'm so excited! I don't know what to do."

"I can see that," responded Ms. Webb with a chuckle. "Maybe you should go and pack. She will be leaving here in less than a week, and your work around here won't be slowing down before you leave." Lillian kissed Ms. Webb on the cheek and ran with haste to her room to start packing. As she was packing, she remembered how Lady Abigail was the one who had interviewed her for the job. Lady Robinson wasn't feeling well that day and had asked Lady Abigail to stand in for her. She knew she wouldn't have gotten the job if Lady Robinson had been the one to interview her because she couldn't even look her in the eyes. Lady Abigail could see that she had no confidence or feelings of self-worth, so she gave her the job and began working with her every day. She had her practice looking into her eyes and holding her head up. "We all have the same Creator, and God is no respecter of persons. He has made no one better than you. Having material things doesn't make one more valuable," Lady Abigail would say. She taught her how to love herself and how to read. In fact she taught several of the servants how to.

The greatest thing she taught her was about God's love for her. Lillian's dad had left her and her mom when Lillian was only a baby. She had never met him or known the love of a man. Her mother worked as many jobs as possible to keep them both alive. As soon as Lillian was old enough to work, she did. She had always been overworked and underappreciated until she had started working for Lady Abigail. Lady Abigail had been better to her than anyone except for her sweet mother, who had passed away three years earlier. She wished many times that her mother could have seen the fancy home she was able to work in, and now she would be working in the palace for the princess. It all seemed too good to be true.

It was Abigail's last day before leaving for the palace. She spent her entire day walking all over the village and speaking to every person she knew. She had one final thing she had to do before leaving the next morning. She had saved it for last. She slowly walked through the churchyard. Behind the church was the cemetery. Memories of Luke's passing and funeral flooded her thoughts. Even though he had been gone for three years, the ache in her heart from missing him never left. She walked over to a tombstone, which read, "Luke Evins, 1892–1915."

Abigail knelt down. "I know you're not here, my love. You are in heaven enjoying Jesus and things that my eyes have not seen and my ears have not heard—things I cannot even imagine. I am here for me. I love you, Luke. I miss you so much. Everywhere I look I have memories of you. It hurts so much that I have to go away. So I'm getting married. I don't love him, and I will never love anyone like I love you. It's like my papa said: love never dies. Even though you are not here, our love remains with each other." Crying, she pulled out a necklace from her bag. She looked down at her engagement ring from Luke. "For the rest of my life, I may not wear it on my finger, but I will wear it next to my heart." She took the ring off her finger; she put it on the necklace and put the necklace around her neck. She stood up, kissed her hand, and touched the tombstone. "Rest in peace, my love." She stood there for a while with tears streaming down her face.

The next morning Abigail woke up before dawn. She had cried a great deal over the past few weeks. She was done with the tears. She was determined to make the most of this new chapter in her life. She couldn't imagine what it would be like, but she knew God was with her, and that was all that mattered. She had chosen the servant Lillian to come with her and serve as her lady's maid. She and Abigail had a good relationship. She was thankful to have a familiar face from home to see every day. As soon as the servants were up, Abigail made her rounds and spoke encouraging words to each one. Lady Robinson was going with Abigail to stay for a couple of weeks to help get her settled in. The servants were very sad to see Abigail leaving. The morning was very somber. Several of the servants were crying. They knew now they would only see her during short visits. Abigail was sad, but she desperately needed a new start—and this was her chance.

Chapter Five

Abigail got out of the car and stood there looking up at the palace. This would be her home for a while. It seemed surreal. She knew she had a lot of hard work ahead of her, but she was ready for the challenge. When she and Lady Robinson walked through the doors of the palace, the king, queen, and prince were there to greet them. The king and queen were beyond excited to see her. Prince Everett had forgotten how beautiful Abigail was. He walked over to her and whispered in her ear, "They haven't stopped smiling since we made our announcement."

"Neither has my grandmother." They laughed.

"We will let you two get settled in, and we'll see you at dinner. Archie will show you to your suite, Lady Abigail. This is where you will be staying until you're married. We'll go over everything tonight at dinner concerning the next month," said the queen.

"Your Majesties," said Lady Robinson and Abigail as they curtsied. They followed Archie. He took Lady Robinson to her room and then Abigail to her suite. Abigail was surprised at the size of it. It was like an apartment. It had a nice bed and sleeping area, a sitting room, and a small kitchenette. Her favorite thing about the suite was the view from her window. It had a wonderful view of the garden. She wished she could continue staying there even after the wedding, but she was sure that wouldn't be an option.

Lillian came into the room. "Do you need anything, milady? Perhaps some tea?"

"No, thank you. How do you like it here so far?"

Lillian's face lit up with sheer joy. "I love it, milady! I feel like I'm in a fairy tale. I keep pinching myself."

Abigail laughed. "I'm glad you're here with me. Why don't you get settled in? I think I will rest before dinner."

"As you wish, milady. I'll be back at seven o'clock to help you change for dinner."

At dinner everyone was joyful. It seemed like a celebration. Everyone except Abigail and Prince Everett was smiling and laughing. Trying to make conversation with Abigail, the prince leaned over and asked, "How have you been since you left here? Have you changed your mind?"

"Honestly, I was more emotional than I would like to admit," said Abigail solemnly.

"Emotional? Like crying?"

"Yes. After the engagement is officially announced,

everyone will know who I am. I, too, will be with you in your fishbowl."

The prince had never thought of how it would affect her. "I'm sorry I've asked so much from you. If you don't want to go through with this, we don't have to," said the prince with concern.

"Is this still what you want, Your Highness?" asked Abigail.

"It is," said Prince Everett with no hesitation.

"You are my future king. I will gladly do this for you—that is, if you still agree with the terms you agreed to."

"I will forever be indebted to you. Shall we have our first date this coming Friday?" asked the prince.

"I would like that. It doesn't have to be long, maybe thirty minutes," said Abigail with a smile."

"I'll be there," responded the prince.

The queen interrupted. "Have you seen your schedule for the month?"

"No, Your Majesty," said Abigail.

"You will start on Monday. There will be long days, but I know you will breeze right through it. The last day of training ends on Friday, February twenty-sixth. We will have a ball to present you to everyone and to announce the engagement. Please make sure you're here for that, Lady Robinson."

"I wouldn't miss it for the world," responded Lady Robinson, who was beaming with pride.

After dinner, the prince walked Abigail to the bottom of the staircase. "I just want to say thank you again for doing this for me. If you change your mind, there will be no hard feelings. No one has ever done anything like this for me."

Abigail gave him a funny look, and they both laughed. The prince corrected himself. "No one has ever done anything so selfless for me."

"I hope it all works out the way your heart desires, Your Highness," said Abigail.

The prince kissed her hand. "I'll see you on Friday." Abigail curtsied and walked up the staircase.

The king walked over to Prince Everett. "She's quite something. I believe you have done very well, Son." The prince didn't say anything as he stood there watching Abigail walk up the stairs.

Monday came, and Abigail was ready for her training. She walked into the dining room for her first lesson. It was to start at breakfast. Today they would go over dining etiquette. Thankfully this would be something Abigail was familiar with. Being from an upper-class family, she had already been trained on what was proper and not. When Abigail entered the room, Ms. Landen came over and introduced herself. She was a tall, thin lady with impeccable poise. Her dark hair was pulled back into a tight bun, and she was strictly business.

"Hello, Lady Abigail. I've heard much about you. Let's get

started. Carry on as you normally would; I will correct you as I see fit."

Abigail had never felt so nervous eating her breakfast. She didn't even feel like eating at that point. She tried not to think about her every move, but it was hard not to do with Ms. Landen literally looking over her shoulder. Was this how the middle class felt when eating a meal with the upper class? *How tragic*, Abigail thought. *It shouldn't be this complicated. It's just eating.*

Apparently Abigail did well. Ms. Landen didn't say anything. Then after a while, she sat down and joined her. "From the time you are announced, Lady Abigail, your every move will be watched and judged. You and your actions will reflect the monarchy. You must do everything with perfection," said Ms. Landen with a stern look in her eye.

Abigail thought of the prince with pity, knowing that his entire life had been filled with this kind of scrutiny. She was even more determined to help him to find happiness. After breakfast, it was time for the next lesson, which was interview etiquette. Ms. Landen gave Abigail some homework to work on for the week. She was to turn it in to her the following Monday.

Abigail's days were filled with one lesson after the next. Ms. Landen was stern and strict. There wasn't a single moment to relax. Every evening after her training, Abigail was very tired. There were so many rules and regulations to remember. *How can etiquette training be this draining?* she thought. *It's not like I'm training for the royal army.* Her days consisted of training all day and then coming back to her room, eating an early dinner, reviewing all that was covered that day, and going to bed. Although it wasn't easy, she pushed through and did her best. She knew it was only a season.

Lillian was eating breakfast with her fellow servants. She was having a hard time fitting in. She hadn't told Lady Abigail because she didn't want to upset her. Lady Abigail was trying to keep her head above water, just getting through training.

"Where did you receive your training to be a lady's maid?" asked Kate with a smirk on her face. She was one of the palace maids.

Lillian hesitated for a second before she answered. "I received my training from Lady Abigail."

"So you had no training at all, and Lady Abigail trained you herself?" Kate looked at Nina with disgust and got up and left the table to start her work for the day.

Bessy, Lillian's roommate and the queen's maid, was sitting beside her. She had been very kind to her. "Don't worry about them. They are just jealous."

"They are right to look down on me. I don't deserve to be here. I never had formal training," said Lillian as she looked down at her plate.

Archie, who had overheard the conversation, sat down across the table from her. "If Lady Abigail chose you to be her maid, then don't let anyone make you feel that you aren't worthy of sitting here."

Lillian smiled timidly at Archie. "Thank you." Lillian didn't feel much like eating, but she ate anyway.

Abigail woke up with excitement. At last it was Friday! She would finally have a couple of days to rest and catch her breath. She was looking forward to walking in the garden again. She had been too tired to do it in the evenings. Tonight she would be seeing the prince for a few minutes. She grabbed a pen and paper and jotted down some questions she needed to know to complete her homework assignment that was due on Monday.

The prince and Andrew were playing croquet on the palace grounds. They played every Friday afternoon when the weather allowed it. "So is Abigail here at the palace?" asked Andrew with curiosity.

"She is. She's been here for a week. She's in etiquette training right now."

"Etiquette training?" said Andrew with a laugh. "So what's that exactly?"

"It's actually quite intense. She's learning proper titles and greetings for now and also for after she becomes a princess. She's learning how to give speeches and conduct herself during interviews, ballroom etiquette and the different types of dances, poise, fashion, and politics," said the prince.

"It sounds grueling. I can't believe she would do all this for you. Like I said there must be an ulterior motive."

"If there is, I have yet to find it," responded the prince.

"So can I meet her?"

"The queen wants her to stay in the palace and remain a secret for the next month. On February twenty-sixth, there will be a ball. You are invited, of course. She'll be presented to everyone, including you, then."

"Why should I have to wait like everyone else? I'm your best friend," asked Andrew.

"I'm not sure. I'm just following the queen's orders," said Prince Everett sarcastically.

Andrew looked up, and there was Abigail, looking out into the garden through the window of her room. She didn't even notice them. "Is that her?" asked Andrew as he pointed to the window.

The prince looked over to where he had pointed, "Yes, that's her. She must be having her lunch."

The two of them just stood there staring at her. "I don't know what she looks like up close, but from here, she's beautiful."

"She's more beautiful close up," responded the prince.

Abigail walked away from the window. "I can see now why the queen wants to keep her in. She doesn't want anyone stealing her away from you." They both laughed and finished their game.

Abigail was sitting at a card table looking over the questions she had written down. The prince walked into the room. Abigail quickly stood up and curtsied. "Your Highness."

"Before we go on any further, I insist that you call me Everett and skip all formalities with me."

"That would contradict everything I've been learning this week," Abigail said with a sarcastic smile.

"Speaking of training, how's everything going?"

"Oh, it's going. I enjoy some of the subjects more than others."

"Which subject is your favorite?" asked the prince.

"Definitely dancing!"

"So you enjoy dancing"

"I do. I've always loved to dance."

"Well, I hope you save a dance or two for me at the ball."

"I'm not sure if I can. I guess I will try to fit you in," said Abigail with a mischievous smile.

He laughed. "So what's this?" asked the prince as he picked up the paper Abigail had been reading when he came into the room.

"I thought you could help me with a homework assignment. I was given a list of some of the questions the reporters might ask at our first interview. I thought we should prepare some of our answers together."

"All right. So what's one of the questions?"

"Where's your favorite place to go? And what things do you like to do?" asked Abigail.

"I love the lakes and mountains. I enjoy fly-fishing and hunting. I really enjoy being outdoors." As Abigail was writing it all down, the prince interrupted her. "Where's your favorite place to go? And what things do you enjoy doing?"

"I love the beach and the ocean. I also love being outdoors. I sometimes feel claustrophobic if I've been inside too long, especially in the winter."

The prince nodded his head in agreement. They went on back and forth with questions. They were surprised by how much they had in common. Abigail looked over at the clock. "I'm so sorry. I told you this would only take thirty minutes, and we went ten minutes over. We can do this another time. Perhaps next Friday," said Abigail as she was collecting all of her things.

"Don't worry about it. I can stay as long as you need. I want to help you with your homework. After all, if it weren't for me, you wouldn't have homework."

Abigail stood up. "I refuse to take any more of your time. I will see you next Friday. Your Highness." She curtsied.

He kissed her hand. "Just Everett." She smiled and left the room.

—————

The second week went a little smoother. Abigail wasn't nearly as tired as she was the first week. She wasn't fond of Ms. Landen, but she had gotten used to her constant correction. Her grandmother went home. She hadn't been able to visit with her much. She had been so busy. Thankfully her grandmother understood and was very supportive and encouraging. She and the queen had been enjoying each other's company. Abigail couldn't believe Friday was already here. She always looked forward to Saturday and Sunday. She was looking out the window, enjoying the scenery, and then noticed the time. She jumped up and ran out the door. She was going to be late for her date with the prince!

When she walked into the room, he was standing there waiting. "I'm so sorry, Your Highness. I lost track of time."

"Please call me Everett. It's all right; I haven't been waiting long. What's our activity for tonight? Do you have more homework for us to work on?"

Abigail laughed at his question. "Well, kind of. I hope you are wearing comfortable shoes. I was told that we will be dancing the first dance together at the ball, so I thought it would be a good idea for us to practice dancing together."

"I definitely agree," said the prince with a smile. He walked over to the Graphophone to play some music. When the music started, he walked over to Abigail and took her hand. "Shall we?" They locked arms and began to dance. Abigail avoided looking into the prince's eyes. He was very handsome. The prince didn't take his eyes off her. After a couple of minutes, he said with a warm smile, "You're quite good."

"You act surprised. I told you I enjoyed dancing."

"Just because you enjoy something doesn't mean you're good at it," said the prince.

"True. You should have heard my papa sing. He enjoyed it, but he was the only one." They laughed. "You're a pretty decent dancer yourself," said Abigail.

"I've had a lot of practice. I've gone to my share of balls. Speaking of balls, are you excited about yours?" asked the prince.

"Mine?" replied Abigail.

"Well, the ball at which you will be introduced."

"I would say more nervous than excited. It's like a final test to see if I passed or failed," said Abigail as she rolled her eyes.

"I have no doubt that everyone will love you. I'm sure of it. You have won over the king and queen, and that's really all that matters."

"They just want you wed. I don't think that it has much to do with me," said Abigail.

"That isn't completely true. I'm sure there would have been some pushback if I had chosen someone on my own."

Abigail looked into the prince's eyes with compassion. "Eventually you are going to choose someone on your own, and you won't have their approval. Maybe we shouldn't go through with this."

"That's not an option. The question is: What if I never find anyone else? Are you willing to stay in this marriage as it is? As merely friends?" asked the prince with concern in his voice.

"I don't think that will happen. I am confident that you will find love," responded Abigail with uncertainty in her heart. He had brought up a concern that she hadn't thought about.

They kept dancing, both in deep thought. "I'm really looking forward to introducing you to my best friend, Lord Macentire—or, to me, Andrew. He can't wait to meet you."

"Does he know about our arrangement?" she asked.

"He does. He doesn't understand it at all, but he doesn't judge us for it."

"I'm sure it would seem crazy to the outside world. Honestly it seems crazy to me," said Abigail with a laugh.

"I know I keep saying it, but thank you, Abigail, for doing this for me. It means more to me than you will ever know."

"You are very welcome," she said with a tender smile. Abigail wanted to change the subject. "I know you say you have a lot of experience with dancing, but do you actually enjoy it?"

The prince gazed into her eyes, "It depends on whom I'm dancing with." They stared into each other's eyes for a moment.

Abigail's heart began to race. She looked away. "I think we've got it. I won't take any more of your time; after all, you actually have a life." She pulled away, walked over, and stopped the music.

"Well, I guess I will see you next Friday. Oh, and next Friday the activity is on me. There's something we have to do before the ball," the prince said with a smile. He took her hand and kissed it. She curtsied, and they went their separate ways.

Chapter Six

Abigail was on her way to the drawing room to meet the prince for their Friday date. She was tired, but she was so excited that she only had one week of training left. She was ready to be able to leave the palace and begin doing the things that she wanted to do. She was planning to volunteer at the hospital and the local orphanage. When she walked into the room, she saw a man surrounded by at least a dozen cases opened with an assortment of the most beautiful rings. She just stood there, unsure of what to do.

Prince Everett walked over and took her hand. "This is Mr. Howard."

Mr. Howard bowed. "Milady."

"He is here to assist you in choosing an engagement and wedding ring," said the prince.

Abigail stopped and looked at different rings. "Please,

milady, feel free to try on as many as you like," said Mr. Howard.

"The last time I was shopping for an engagement ring, I tried to choose the least expensive ring because I knew Luke didn't have much money. He didn't come from a family with money like you and I. Believe it or not, that was one of the many things I loved about him. I would have wrapped a wire around my finger if it came down to it because his love for me exceeded the cost of any ring. Here I am, surrounded by the most exquisite and expensive rings that money can buy, and I can have my choice of any of them, but it really doesn't mean anything. Life can be so crazy," said Abigail with discouragement in her voice as she walked around the cases of rings.

After looking at every ring and not trying a single one of them on, she made her way over to the door. She looked up at the prince, "They are all very beautiful. You can choose one. It's just a ring."

She turned to Mr. Howard. "Thank you for your time," she said politely. She curtsied to the prince. "Your Highness." She walked out the door.

The prince stood there, confused about what had just happened, "Well, that didn't go as I expected."

Lillian was walking down the hall with her arms full of laundry. Archie passed by and smiled, and she smiled back while they both kept walking. "Lillian!"

She turned around, and Archie was holding a piece of laundry she had apparently dropped. Embarrassed, she walked over to him, "Thank you," she said as she took it from his hand. Their hands brushed against each other. She blushed. He smiled at her and kept walking. She stood there for a second and then went on her way.

― ―

A week later, Abigail danced to her room. She was very excited that her training was complete! She was nervous about the ball that night, but there would be dancing, and she loved to dance. She was made aware of how the evening would flow. First there would be a greeting from the king and queen. They would make her introduction and then announce the engagement. Then she and the prince would come out and dance their first dance together. The rest of the night would be spent meeting people and dancing. She was looking forward to the night being over, but she would make the most of it.

After Abigail was dressed and had put on her gloves, Lillian stepped back from the mirror to look at Abigail. "Oh my stars! I've never seen someone so beautiful, milady! You truly look like a princess."

"Well, let's hope I can act like one," said Abigail with doubt in her voice.

"If they only knew your heart like I do, they would love you unconditionally."

"Unfortunately, Lillian, if they truly did know me and how I loathe the ways of the upper class and all their formalities, they would feel the opposite. That's why this is so hard for me. I feel like I'm being fake," said Abigail.

"Well, maybe you can help change things for the better once you are the princess of Noreland," said Lillian with pride.

"If I had it my way, Lillian, you would be on that dance floor dancing with me."

"That sounds wonderful, milady, but for now you will have to dance for the both of us. Is there anything else you need, milady, before I leave you?"

"Prayers. Lots and lots of prayers." They both laughed.

"I will say a prayer for you, milady. I can't wait to hear about everything later tonight when I help you get ready for bed."

Abigail took in a deep breath and sighed. She slowly walked out of her door and to the stairs, pausing before she went down. From the top of the staircase, she saw the prince waiting for her at the bottom. He seemed so calm and composed. Halfway down the stairs, Abigail and the prince made eye contact and gazed into each other's eyes, admiring each other's appearance. When she reached the bottom of the stairs, she curtsied. "Your Highness."

"You look stunning, Abigail," said the prince.

"Thank you. You look very nice also."

They walked into a small waiting room. The king and

queen would be making the announcement at any time. They would soon be going out for their first dance. The prince couldn't stop staring at her.

"I wanted to apologize for last Friday. The hardest thing I've had to do through this entire process has been removing my engagement ring from my finger, especially for one that really has no meaning behind it," said Abigail.

"There is no need for you to apologize. I'm sorry that I was too selfish to see it from your perspective." The prince took her hand and placed an engagement ring on her finger. "I chose this ring because it reminded me of you. The blue stone reminded me of your eyes. It's beautiful yet simple and not flashy. I hope you like it."

Abigail looked down at the ring and smiled. "You chose well."

Just then Archie walked into the room. "It's time."

They looked into each other's eyes. The prince could see that Abigail was nervous. "Just follow my lead. I've got you." The prince took her by the hand and walked her out, and they stood in front of a large crowd. Everyone was applauding and cheering. The music began. They locked arms and began to dance. Abigail followed his lead. As long as she kept her eyes on him, her nervousness subsided.

He was strong, confident, and unshakable. She had thought that he would be arrogant and selfish before they met. She was finding him to be reliable, kind, and thoughtful. She wouldn't dare entertain the thought of herself falling for him, but she knew that whomever he chose would be a very fortunate lady.

The dance was over. They stood there a moment, looking into each other's eyes. Everyone applauded and cheered. They walked off the dance floor while others walked onto it. Another song started.

"Before you venture off, I have to introduce you to Andrew." Andrew was walking toward them. "Lady Abigail, I would like you to meet Lord Macentire."

Abigail curtsied. "Lord Macentire, it's nice to meet you."

"Please call me Andrew; we are practically family. May I have this dance with the most beautiful woman here?"

"How could I refuse an offer like that?" said Abigail as she took his hand, and they walked to the dance floor.

"Prince Everett and I are like brothers. We have been since we were lads."

"Then please call me Abigail. I suppose you have some embarrassing stories you could share about the prince."

"Oh yes. I could keep you entertained all evening," responded Andrew.

The two of them laughed. Prince Everett was watching them dance and laugh. He felt a slight twinge of jealousy. He shook it off and began dancing with Lady Edith. She was beautiful but loved herself more than anyone else. Prince Everett saw right through it.

Abigail and Andrew got along very well. When they finished their dance, before Abigail walked off, Andrew stopped her.

"I know you don't have any family or friends around here. If you need anything, please don't hesitate to ask."

"Thank you. And thank you for the dance," responded Abigail with a smile.

The queen came over and began introducing Abigail to several different people. Abigail played her part well. She pleased the king and queen with how she represented herself. Abigail also danced with several different people throughout the night. Every time she was on the dance floor, the prince was dancing with a different lady. She kept wondering if he were interested in any of them and why someone so handsome, kind, and desirable would be in this kind of arrangement.

It was getting late, and the ball was coming to an end. Abigail was exhausted, but she had held her own and put on a good show. She excused herself with the king and queen and left the ballroom. She began walking up the stairs.

"Abigail!"

She turned around, and the prince was walking toward her. "I apologize, Your Highness. I didn't see you, or I would have excused myself," said Abigail.

"I just wanted to tell you that you did wonderful tonight. If it were a pass or fail, you definitely passed. When it comes to your beauty, you were the most beautiful lady here."

She blushed. "Thank you, Your Highness, for your kind words. I suppose I will see you next Friday." She smiled and continued up the stairs.

Abigail was eating breakfast the next morning in her room.

Lillian walked in with overwhelming excitement. "Milady, the papers are raving about you! The people love you! You made a wonderful impression last night. Would you like to read about it?" She handed Abigail the newspaper.

"That's all right, Lillian. Thank you for your enthusiasm, but I was only playing a role. I didn't even want to be there with those types of people who love themselves mostly, their money, and their class. However, God loves them as much as he loves me, so I will choose to love them also."

Lillian picked up a hairbrush and began brushing Abigail's hair. "So what are your plans today, milady, now that you can go out of the palace and see the city?"

"I'm going to stay in for the weekend. I want to walk in the garden and rest. Monday, I plan to go to the hospital to see when and if I can start volunteering, and Tuesday, I plan on going to the orphanage to do the same. After that, we'll see. I'm sure I will be given a schedule with my royal obligations and duties. Then there are the wedding plans."

"There are reporters surrounding the palace, waiting to get a picture and glimpse of you."

"They will soon be bored and tired of me. Unlike the prince, I don't attend parties and put myself in places that give them leverage to write about."

"Maybe with their eyes on you, they will let up on the prince for a while," said Lillian.

"That's what I'm hoping for. I want the prince to be happy. The more I'm submerged in this life, the more I realize the difficulties he's had to endure. In a lot of ways, he's lived a hard life, and I greatly desire his happiness. Enough about me. How have you been, Lillian? Do you still like it here?"

Lillian hesitated. "I don't exactly fit in. Most of the staff have formal training, and I...well, you know my inadequacies."

Abigail stood up, turned toward Lillian, and looked her in the eyes. "Do not let yourself go back to your old way of thinking. Look how far you've come! You deserve to be here as much as anyone else. God is the one who ordains our paths. There is no one here better than you, Lillian. You mustn't let anyone make you feel differently."

"Thank you, milady. You are one of the few people in this world who believe in me," said Lillian with her eyes looking down.

"Look into my eyes. You don't need anyone to believe in you, Lillian. You just need to believe in yourself."

Just then there was a knock at the door. Lillian and Abigail looked at the door. "Come in."

The door opened, and it was Archie. He stepped in and bowed. "Milady, His Royal Highness has asked if you would attend church with him tomorrow."

Abigail smiled. "Tell him I would be delighted to,"

"Very well, milady." Archie looked at Lillian and smiled. Lillian blushed. He left the room and closed the door.

"Are the two of you courting?" asked Abigail.

"No, milady, but I do find him quite attractive, and he's one of the few here who has been kind to me."

Abigail smiled. "Will you be attending church tomorrow, Lillian?"

"I was planning to," answered Lillian.

"Well, perhaps Archie would like to come with you," Abigail said with a mischievous smile.

"Perhaps he would, milady."

"You'll never know unless you ask."

Lillian left Abigail's room, trying to work up the courage to ask Archie to go to church with her the next day.

As soon as Abigail left the palace and entered the church, the motive behind the invitation to church was crystal clear. Reporters were everywhere, and the bright-white flashes were blinding. Abigail and the prince didn't speak much before the service. Abigail loathed all of the attention, but she knew it came with the territory. After her newness wore off, she hoped she would get less attention. After the service was over, Abigail and Prince Everett walked out of the church. Trying to ignore the reporters, the prince asked, "Did you enjoy the service?"

"I did. How about you?"

"I don't know if I totally agree that joy can only be found in God," exclaimed the prince with a smirk on his face.

"I disagree with you. I do feel joy can only come from God," she said as she stopped walking. She turned and looked into his eyes and continued, "I think you are confusing joy with happiness. Happiness is fleeting. It comes and goes. It's based on what is happening to us and around us. It's self-centered. Joy, on the other hand, is something we can only obtain from God. It's something we have, regardless of what is happening. It's selfless. It comes from serving Him and serving others. Think about it like this. Everything in this world is constantly changing. We are constantly changing. We think, 'If I had this or that, then I would be happy.' Then we get whatever it is, and we're quickly bored with it and off to the next thing. Relationships can bring happiness, but they can't bring joy.

"Eventually the other person will hurt or frustrate you. They are flawed because they are merely human. True and meaningful happiness does come only from a relationship with Jesus, who gives an unchanging joy and peace that you have, even when you don't have things that you want or life is not going the way that you think it should. Is the reason you haven't found love, because you're looking for a woman to bring you joy? A significant other can add to your happiness, but they can't be the source of it." Abigail had hardly taken a breath.

"Ah! I've just heard two sermons in one day." They both laughed. "Maybe you should preach next Sunday," said the prince sarcastically.

"Maybe I will," said Abigail with a smile as they kept walking to the car.

Prince Everett was quiet on the way home. He kept thinking about what Abigail had said. Maybe the reason he hadn't married was that he was looking for a woman to be the source of his happiness. He had enjoyed the company of some of the most beautiful women in the country. Maybe the fault was with him. Maybe he had blown his chance at finding love.

Before Abigail got out of the car, Prince Everett stopped her. "This Friday we have an interview with a reporter from the newspaper. It will be held in the drawing room at seven p.m."

"Our first interview. I hope we're ready. I'll see you on Friday," she said as she got out of the car. The prince watched her until she walked into the palace, and he rode off.

Lillian walked into Abigail's room to help her change for dinner. "You look sad, milady. How did things go today?"

"I am a little disheartened. I went to the hospital today to see if I could volunteer as a nurse, and they denied me. They said there's a Spanish flu going around, and many people have died from it. Because of my close proximity to the king, queen, and prince, they wouldn't let me."

"I'm sorry, milady. I know how much you enjoy working in the hospital."

"It's all right. They are right. I would never want to jeopardize their health or well-being. Enough about me. Did you ask Archie to go to church on Sunday?"

"I wanted to, but I couldn't find the courage. He's very handsome, and I couldn't. What if he had said no?"

"Then he would have said no, and you would have survived it and gone on your way. He's no better looking than you. Ask him this Sunday."

"We'll see, milady. I wish he would ask me." Before Lillian left Abigail's room, she turned around and said, "Thank you for giving me Sundays off, milady. It really means a lot to me."

"You are very welcome, Lillian. Thank you for being such a wonderful maid and friend." Lillian curtsied and left the room.

The prince and Andrew were playing their weekly game of croquet. "Lady Abigail looked stunning at the ball. I can see why you and the country are so taken by her. I don't know how you think you will be able to find a wife when you have someone so close to perfection right in front of you."

The prince sighed. "She's made her feelings very clear. She never intends to give her heart to anyone else. I accept that. So for the time being, I will enjoy her friendship until I find someone."

Andrew shook his head in disbelief. "You're a stronger man than I."

The prince was agitated with Andrew's great admiration of Abigail. He knew it was a moot point, so he brushed it off.

Abigail was elated as she walked out of the orphanage. She was so happy she didn't even notice the photographers and flashes as she made her way to the car. She was going to start the next day and work every Monday, Wednesday, and Friday that didn't interfere with her royal affairs. Finally she was going to get to do something that she wanted to do.

The next day, Abigail walked into the orphanage and was put at a desk organizing mail. She was finished in about thirty minutes and just sat there. She looked down the hall. There was a maid with a cart. She was pushing a large load of dirty laundry. Abigail jumped up and followed her to a large room, where two other women were scrubbing, rinsing, and hanging laundry to dry. When Abigail walked into the room, they stopped and curtsied. They had looks of fear on their faces. "Milady."

"Hello. I'm Abigail. I came here to work and help out however I can. I can see you have a lot of work to do. Can I help you, ladies?"

"Oh no, milady. You are to be a princess, and your clothes are too nice for this kind of work. You will get dirty."

"What's your name?" asked Abigail.

"My name is Ruth, milady."

"I am no better than you, Ruth. These clothes can be washed or even replaced. Please, I insist. Let me help."

Ruth hesitated at first. "As you wish, milady. You can hang the clothes up after they've been washed.

"Thank you," said Abigail as she went to work.

After they worked for about thirty minutes, the headmistress came into the laundry room. "Milady, I've been looking for you everywhere! What are you doing? Ruth, how could you have put her to work?"

Abigail interrupted her. "Ms. Myers, I came here to work, not just to sit here and look pretty. These ladies were working hard, and I insisted on helping them."

"But you are to be the princess," said Ms. Myers.

"But I am Abigail now and forever. I am a Christian called to serve like everyone else. Please, Ms. Myers, let me serve."

Surprised by Abigail's rebuttal, she said, "As you wish, milady. Would you like to meet the children on Friday? They are doing their lessons right now, or I would introduce you."

"I would love that! Thank you, Ms. Myers," said Abigail with complete excitement.

On Friday, Abigail went to the orphanage. Reporters took pictures and shouted for her attention the entire way. She learned to just smile and wave. She never read the newspapers. As long as she was true to God and to herself, she didn't care what people said or thought about her.

When Abigail walked in the door, Ms. Myers was there to greet her, "Good morning, milady." She curtsied.

"Good morning, Ms. Myers."

"The children are very excited to meet you."

"I am very excited to meet them," responded Abigail with a huge smile on her face.

"Please follow me." Abigail followed her into a large

dining area with four long tables. The children were sitting, eating their breakfast. When they saw her, they all stood up. The girls curtsied, and the boys bowed.

"Good morning, children. It is my pleasure to meet you. My name is Abigail. I am hoping to get to know each of you over the next few days."

A little girl around seven years old raised her hand. "Yes, sweetheart?"

"Are you a real princess?"

"I am not a princess yet. After I marry the prince in about three weeks, I will be a real princess."

Another little girl raised her hand. "Yes?" said Abigail.

"You are very beautiful."

"Thank you. You are very beautiful also," Abigail responded.

"Everyone, finish eating so you can do your chores and get to your schooling," said Ms. Myers.

A little girl around four years old walked over to Abigail, grabbed her hand, and looked up at her, "Will you be my mommy?"

Trying to hold back tears, Abigail knelt down and looked into the little girl's eyes and said, "I would love to be your mommy, but I'm not able to. However, I would love to be your very special friend. Can I be your very special friend?"

The little girl's eyes lit up. "I would like that."

"What's your name, sweetheart?"

"Ruby."

"It's official. We are special friends," exclaimed Abigail as she held out her hand to shake on it. The little girl got a huge smile on her face and hugged Abigail instead. She hugged her so tightly. Abigail's heart ached at the thought of this child never knowing the love of a mother or a father and knowing that she would never have children of her own or even be able to adopt. She was determined not to show her emotions and to make the most of every moment she had with these children. She played games with them, sang with them, and danced with them.

She left the orphanage with a bag full of pictures and crafts the children had given her throughout the day. Her favorite part of her day was making a special friendship. She felt so incredibly blessed as she was walking into the palace heading toward the study, where she and the prince were to be interviewed.

When she walked through the door, the prince said, "You're beaming! What did you do today?"

"I spent my entire day at the orphanage." She started showing him some of the pictures and crafts from her bag.

"They seem to love you, just like everyone else," exclaimed the prince as he looked over the artwork she was showing him.

"No, their love isn't like everyone else's. Their love is genuine. They love me for me."

The reporter walked into the room and bowed, "Your Highness, milady. Shall we begin?"

Everyone sat down. The reporter took out some paper

and a pen and cleared his throat, "Your Highness, you have a reputation of entertaining many beautiful women over the years. My question is: Why Lady Abigail?"

The prince looked at Abigail as if he were embarrassed. "Abigail is different from every lady I've ever met. Not only is she incredibly beautiful, he's also kind and genuine. She understands me."

The reporter went back and forth, asking them both questions. "Last question. Lady Abigail, what's your favorite quality about the prince?"

She looked over at the prince. "He keeps his word, and he accepts me for who I am and doesn't try and change me."

"Same question to you, Your Highness. What's your favorite quality about Lady Abigail?"

The prince looked into Abigail's eyes. "She's loyal, confident, and puts others above herself. I am very grateful to have her in my life." The prince and Abigail looked into each other's eyes for a moment. Abigail quickly looked away.

"If that concludes our interview, then I should be going." She stood and looked at the prince and curtsied. "Your Highness."

Chapter Seven

Abigail was meeting with the queen and the wedding planner. "It's hard to believe the big day is tomorrow!" said the queen with a huge smile on her face. Just then there was a knock on the door. "Come in," responded the queen.

Her private secretary walked in with a grim look on his face. He bowed. "Your Majesty, may I please have a word with you in private?"

Abigail and the wedding planner stood up and walked to the door. "Don't go too far. I will call you back in a moment." They stepped out.

Abigail was concerned about the news the queen might be receiving. By the look on the private secretary's face, it didn't seem good. After a few minutes, they were called back in. The queen had tears in her eyes. "I just received word that my brother died unexpectedly only an hour ago."

"Shouldn't we postpone the wedding?" asked Abigail.

"You need to go to the prince and sort things out with him. I'm sure he will be very upset when he receives the news. He and his uncle were very close."

Abigail curtsied. "If you will excuse me, I need to go and find him."

Abigail searched all over the palace and couldn't find him anywhere; then she remembered she hadn't checked in the gardens. When she walked out, she saw him sitting alone on a bench with tears running down his cheeks. When he saw her, he quickly wiped his face. She sat down beside him, putting her arms around him.

"I take it you heard the news?"

"I was with the queen when she was told. She mentioned the two of you were very close."

"He was like a father to me. When I was growing up, my parents were obviously very busy. But he always had time for me. He's the one who took me fishing as a boy."

"I'm so sorry, Everett. I know the pain of losing someone you love. I wouldn't wish it upon anyone, especially not someone that I care about."

"Well, since we are to marry tomorrow, it's nice to hear that you care about me," said the prince with a smile. They both laughed.

"Do you still want to carry on with the wedding, or should we postpone it?"

"Oh, we're not postponing it. If we did, you might change your mind." They laughed again.

"No, seriously. If you decide that would be best, then—"

He interrupted her. "I'm not going to change my mind."

Abigail stood up. "I will let you have some time to yourself. If you need to talk, please know that I'm here for you."

The prince grabbed her hand. "Do you know what upsets me the most about my uncle passing? He never got to meet you. I know that he would have loved you."

Abigail patted his shoulder. "Perhaps we will meet another time in a much better place."

"Perhaps."

As the wedding rehearsal was wrapping up, the prince pulled Abigail aside. "Can we talk for a second?"

"Absolutely!" They walked into a small room off from the sanctuary for some privacy.

"I know you've been concerned about what we're going to do about the honeymoon. I think I have a solution on how to get out of it. You know how my uncle, Lord Abelin, passed this morning. The queen insisted we are together for our wedding night. We will have to share a room only for that night. I will sleep on the floor, and then I will be on my way the next morning. I will be gone for a week. We will just keep putting it off, and it will never happen."

Abigail was relieved. It had been bothering her. "I am very sorry for your loss. I know the two of you had a close relationship."

Prince Everett looked down with a sad look on his face. "Thank you. He will certainly be missed." Trying to change the subject, the prince continued. "I know things are becoming more real. To ease my mind, I need to know if you are still willing to go through with this?"

Abigail paused for a second. "I am if it's what you truly want."

Without hesitation the prince exclaimed, "It is. Thank you, Abigail, for doing this. You are truly an amazing woman. I am privileged to know you."

"I appreciate your kind words, but they are unnecessary, Your Highness. I just hope you find the love and happiness your heart longs for," responded Abigail with a smile.

"Now, because of you, I have a chance." Prince Everett could tell that something else was bothering her. She still seemed uncertain even after the solution to the honeymoon. "Is there something bothering you, Abigail?"

Embarrassed, she looked down. The prince lifted her chin with his hand. "What is it, Abigail? You can tell or ask me for anything."

She paused for a moment. "Our kiss tomorrow. Everyone will be watching, and I'm nervous that it will be a disaster." The prince laughed. Abigail continued. "I don't have as much experience as you. I've only ever kissed Luke."

Trying to hold back a smile, he took her hands. "Would you feel better if we had a practice kiss now? It would be only for practice to ease your mind about tomorrow."

Abigail broke eye contact. The prince had never seen her so vulnerable. He found it endearing. "Perhaps that would be a good idea," said Abigail with embarrassment. Surprised at her response, he stepped closer to her. They looked into each other's eyes. He slowly leaned in closer and closer. Just before his lips touched hers, Abigail pulled back. "I think we'll be fine," she said abruptly.

"Are you sure?"

"I'm sure," said Abigail.

"Very well. In that case I'll see you tomorrow." He took her hand and kissed it. Abigail stood there a moment to collect herself before she walked out.

That night Abigail didn't get much sleep. She tossed and turned. She questioned whether she should go through with it. She was nervous about the ceremony and the kiss and all the people watching. She was also very nervous about the wedding night. How could she let a prince sleep on the floor? So many different thoughts were going through her head. She finally was able to fall asleep for what seemed like only a few minutes before Lillian was pulling back the curtains.

"Good morning, milady. Today is your wedding day!"

When Abigail heard those words, her heart dropped into her stomach. She sat up in bed; her head was throbbing from the lack of sleep and worry. "I don't feel like eating breakfast this morning. I don't have much of an appetite."

"I understand, milady. Please try and eat as much as you can. You will need extra strength for today...and for tonight," said Lillian with mischief in her voice. Abigail gave Lillian a look of aggravation.

Abigail was very quiet the entire morning. Lillian had never seen her so reserved and nervous. "I will be back around five to help you get ready for the wedding." Abigail just sat there quietly. Lillian walked over and hugged Abigail. "Everything will be perfect, milady."

"Thank you, Lillian." Lillian left the room. Abigail sat down at her small table and tried eating a little but wasn't able to. She felt like she wouldn't be able to keep it down.

Lillian put the veil on Abigail and stepped back to admire her beauty. "Oh, milady! You look gorgeous! You truly look like a princess." Lillian had tears in her eyes. "I'm so happy for you. You deserve this more than anyone. You deserve all the happiness this world has to offer."

Abigail put her hands on Lillian's shoulders. "Thank you. Thank you for always encouraging me. You are not just my maid, but you're a dear friend. I am blessed to have you in this season of my life," said Abigail.

"After tonight I will no longer call you milady but Your Highness."

Abigail looked down. "I haven't thought about that. I guess I have a lot of changes coming my way. Regardless, none of the changes will change me or our friendship."

I'll See You on Friday

Lillian smiled. "Tonight I won't be helping you get ready for bed since it's your wedding night."

Abigail took in a deep breath. Lillian could see that Abigail was very nervous. "Just think...in a few hours, it will all be over. Try to enjoy it and savor the day. Besides, it's only natural for a man and a woman to—"

Abigail stopped her. "Because you are my friend you should know, this marriage is not for love but a favor to the prince."

There was a knock at the door. "Come in," said Abigail.

A servant walked in. "Your Royal Majesties have asked for an audience with you before heading to the church, milady."

"Tell them I will be right down."

"Very well." He left the room.

Lillian walked to the door. "For the last time"—she curtsied—"milady." They smiled at each other with admiration, and Lillian left. Abigail looked at herself in the mirror for a second. She took a deep breath, stood up straight, and walked out the door.

Abigail was announced and walked into the private chambers of the king and queen and curtsied. "Your Majesties."

When they saw her, the queen gasped. "You look beautiful, Abigail. You were meant to be a princess. The prince is a very lucky man to have found you. We also feel fortunate to have you as our daughter-in-law—and, God willing, the mother of our grandchildren and future king."

With tears in her eyes, Abigail said, "Thank you, Your Majesty. I feel that I am the fortunate one. I've never had much of a family, and I feel honored to be becoming a part of yours." Abigail felt guilt and sorrow, knowing that she wouldn't be the mother of their grandchildren. Yet she was confident that whomever the prince chose to give his heart to would be worthy of it. The king and queen would learn to love her, and she would only be a vague memory.

"Now let's go make you an official princess," said the queen.

As Abigail was on her way to the church, she was amazed at all of the people standing on both sides of the street. There were hundreds of people cheering and waving at her. She read many signs that people were holding up, reading, "WE LOVE YOU, ABIGAIL!" It was all so surreal. She felt incredibly blessed. She knew this chapter in her life would be short-lived, but she intended to enjoy every minute and to do as much good as she possibly could.

When Abigail got out of the car, she heard roars, screams, shouting, and cheers. She turned around and waved in all directions. She then bowed her head and said a prayer. "Father, I am your humble servant. Help me to always do your will and represent you to these people for as long as you want. In Jesus's name, I pray. Amen." She took a deep breath and entered the church.

She could hear beautiful music playing. The church seemed so grand and magnificent. She stood there with her heart racing, ready for the double doors to open and to walk down the aisle. Her grandmother walked in through a side door. "My darling! You are so beautiful!" She was wiping tears from her eyes. "I feel very honored to be the one who gets to walk you down the aisle and give you away."

Abigail was breaking tradition by having her grandmother walk her down the aisle. With her papa being gone and the only other male she was close to being Luke's father, it only seemed right for it to be her grandmother. No one seemed to be bothered by her choice, but even if they had been, Abigail would have chosen her grandmother. Lady Robinson couldn't stop the tears. Abigail wanted to tell her grandmother not to cry. It wouldn't be long until she would be back home with her, and things would be back to normal. She knew she couldn't say anything like that at the moment with so many people around, so she leaned over and kissed her on the cheek. "I love you, Grandmother. You know you are always welcome to stay at the palace as long as you would like. I will visit you. This is not goodbye."

The music changed to the wedding march. Lady Robinson patted Abigail's hand, dried her tears, and stood up straight. The double doors opened, and they both began to walk down the very long aisle. Abigail was very thankful to have her grandmother beside her. She had always been there for her. She gazed at the prince as they were walking. He was incredibly handsome. He made her heart race even faster than it already was. She tried not to look his way, but her eyes were drawn to him. She wondered what he was thinking and whether he was as nervous as she was.

When they reached the end of the aisle, the minister asked, "Who gives this bride away?"

With tears, Lady Robinson answered, "I do." She lifted Abigail's veil back, kissed her on the cheek, joined Abigail's hand to Prince Everett's, and sat down.

When they touched, and he saw her incredible beauty, he could hardly breathe. She was better than any woman he could ever have dreamed of. He wished time could stand still for a moment. They went through the service and said their vows. Then the minister said, "I now pronounce you man and wife. You may kiss your bride."

His heart racing, Everett leaned over and gently kissed Abigail. They both felt something they had never felt before. There was overwhelming chemistry between them. When they pulled back, they looked into each other's eyes, wondering if the other had felt the same thing. "What God has joined together, let no man put asunder," said the minister.

Prince Everett and Princess Abigail began walking down the aisle. The crowd was cheering and applauding. When they got to the back of the church, Andrew leaned over and whispered into Prince Everett's ear, "I've never envied you more than I do right now, at this moment." The prince didn't know how to respond to his comment.

They walked out of the church and got into a car, headed

back to the palace for the reception. On the way, there were people shouting, "We love you, Princess Abigail!"

"Princess Abigail!" said the prince.

"It's going to take me a while to get used to being called that," said Abigail.

They were silent for a bit, and then the prince looked at Abigail. "You look stunning. I've never seen a more beautiful bride. Thank you for doing this for me."

Princess Abigail blushed. "You look very handsome yourself. You don't have to keep thanking me. I genuinely want you to be happy and to experience true love one day. Do you have any prospects?"

"I haven't really been looking," answered Prince Everett.

"Well, you better get started. Your Majesties mentioned grandchildren to me earlier today."

"They don't waste any time, do they?" responded the prince. They both laughed.

At the reception Princess Abigail and Prince Everett seemed to talk to everyone except each other. They kept glancing at each other. Every time one would notice the other, they would look away. "It seems things have changed since the engagement. The two of you sure seem to be truly in love," said Lady Robinson with a smile.

"Nothing has changed, Grandmother. We just know each other a little better now, that's all."

"Are you nervous about tonight?"

"A little," said Princess Abigail.

"It's only normal to be nervous. I was nervous on my wedding night. There's no need to be nervous. When you love someone, everything just comes naturally. Just look at the animals. No one has taught them what to do. It's in their instincts, just like it's in yours."

"Grandmother!" said Princess Abigail with embarrassment, trying to keep her voice down to prevent drawing attention. "I appreciate the talk, but it's not needed. Nothing is going to happen, for one, and I am a nurse. I understand how things work."

"Things can always change, darling. He's quite a catch. As time goes on, and whatever happens between the two of you, please know I'm always here for you if you need anything. Marriage isn't always easy, even when there's great love."

Abigail leaned over and kissed her grandmother on the cheek. "I love you, Grandmother. I'm very thankful for you. Thank you for always being there and supporting me through all the good times and the bad. You've been more of a mother to me than a grandmother."

"And you are more like a daughter. The best daughter anyone could ever have. You helped me keep going when I lost your father." She paused for a second, trying not to cry. "I sure wish he could be here to see you today."

Tears welled up in Princess Abigail's eyes.

"Enough about that. Today is your wedding day! What a wonderful day it has been! The best part is yet to come."

"Oh, Grandmother! The way you talk, I'm surprised you

only had one child," said Princess Abigail. The two ladies were laughing when the prince walked up.

"Everyone is ready to see us off. Shall we go?" He held out his arm for her to grab onto.

She leaned down and hugged her grandmother. Lady Robinson whispered into Princess Abigail's ear, "Whatever happens tonight is acceptable in the eyes of God because you are married."

Princess Abigail's eyes widened as she gave an embarrassed look at her grandmother. She grabbed onto the prince's arm, and they walked out the doors while everyone was cheering and clapping to send them off. They didn't say anything on their way to their suite.

When they opened the door to the suite, they saw that it was a small room with a very large bed. Nightclothes laid, folded, on the bed for both of them. There was a bottle of wine and two glasses on a nightstand. "Well, it's obvious what we are expected to do tonight. I'm surprised they even laid out bedclothes," said the prince.

Abigail laughed. "I'm truly very sorry about the loss of your uncle. However, the timing did help out with our predicament."

"I'm glad something good came from it," said Prince Everett as he began taking pillows and covers to make a bed for himself on the floor.

"Do you mind turning around while I change for bed?" asked Princess Abigail.

The prince turned around. His heart began to race. Princess Abigail tried and struggled, but she couldn't get the buttons unbuttoned that ran down the back of her dress. "Is everything all right?" he asked.

"I'm having trouble with unbuttoning some buttons," said Princess Abigail with frustration in her voice.

"Would you like some help?"

She kept trying for a couple of more minutes. Then, with a sigh, she said, "I'm sorry to ask this of you, but do you mind unbuttoning the buttons down my back? I can do the rest."

The prince turned around, and Princess Abigail backed up to him. He paused for a second. His heart began racing even faster. He began slowly unbuttoning the dress. He couldn't take his eyes off the back of her neck. As he was unbuttoning, he got a glimpse of her back. Her skin looked so smooth and soft. It took every ounce of his strength to stop himself from bending down and kissing her.

After he had unbuttoned the dress, he stood there a moment. Princess Abigail turned around and took her hair down. They were face to face. She looked at the prince's mouth and back into his eyes. Fighting the urge to kiss him, she said in a halfhearted way, "Do you mind turning around?"

Prince Everett stared at her. He had never seen anyone look more beautiful than Princess Abigail at that moment, with her long dark hair draping over her shoulders and her big blue eyes. He slowly turned around. His fists clenched.

Holding his breath he fought back the feelings of passion that were swelling up inside him.

Abigail quickly changed and jumped into bed, pulling the covers up to her shoulders. "I will cover my eyes so that you can change." She put the covers over her face. The prince changed and laid down on the bed he had made on the floor. Abigail turned off the light. Princess Abigail lay there, feeling guilty about allowing the prince to sleep on the floor. "Please let me sleep on the floor."

"Absolutely not!" said Prince Everett with sternness in his voice.

"But you are a prince."

"And you are a princess."

"Not really," she said.

"For the time being, you are a princess. And princess or not, I would never allow a lady to lie on the floor while I slept in a bed."

As the prince lay there, looking at the ceiling, he asked, "What qualities do you recommend when looking for a wife?"

Princess Abigail wondered why he would ask her this question. She thought for a second before responding. "Well, the first thing I would recommend is someone who is like-minded in your faith. For me I would want to marry someone who is a Christian. Because of our faith, we would share similar standards and goals. When things get tough—which they would, because it's real life—we would be more likely to stick with it and make better choices because of our higher commitment to God. The second quality I would recommend is marrying your best friend to ensure your marriage is full of laughter and fun. The looks and attraction will fade due to the cruelty of aging, but if you marry your best friend, none of that matters. You will always have loyalty and trust. To sum it all up, I would say you want to marry the person that you want to wake up to every morning. The last face you want to see at night. The first person you want to tell when you receive good news. The person whose arms can bring the most comfort when you're down. The person who is in your corner and will stand with you when no one else will. The person whom you feel as though you can't live without."

Everett was overwhelmed by her wisdom at such a young age. "Are those the qualities you found in Luke?"

Princess Abigail was silent and then answered hesitantly, "Yes. All of them."

"He was a very fortunate man to have had your heart."

"I believe I was the fortunate one," she responded.

"Are you still set on never marrying again?"

"I don't think it's likely, but then again, with God, all things are possible."

"So what's changed your mind?"

"I never said my mind has changed. I'm just saying I'm open for God to change it." There was silence for a minute. "So what is it that you are looking for in a wife?"

"Honestly, there have not been any set qualities. I just want to be the one to choose whom I marry. I want her to love me for me and not because I'm a prince. I want to love her more than anyone else in the world and for her to love me the same."

"I genuinely hope you find all your heart desires. I suppose we should try and get some sleep, especially with you having to get up so early."

"I will try my best not to wake you in the morning. I'll see you next Friday," said the prince.

"Good night," said Princess Abigail as she rolled over onto her side and adjusted her pillows to go to sleep. Neither of them slept much that night. They couldn't stop thinking about each other.

When Everett got up the next morning, he tried to be quiet and not wake Princess Abigail as he dressed and collected his things. Before he left the room, he stopped and stared at her. He watched her sleep. She was so beautiful. He couldn't deny his growing feelings for her. He knew her feelings weren't the same for him. He knew it would be hard, but he had to think of her only as a friend.

Chapter Eight

The prince walked into his new room after returning from his uncle's funeral. He couldn't wait to see Abigail. He hadn't stopped thinking about her the entire time he was gone. He heard her voice and realized there was an adjoining door to his room. He eagerly opened the door. There she was, as beautiful as ever, sitting on her love seat, meeting with her private secretary. She looked over at him with a flirtatious smile. "Well, hello, stranger. It's nice to see you're back."

Her secretary excused himself and left the room. "How did everything go?"

"As good as any funeral could go, I guess."

"I'm sorry. That was a terrible question," said Princess Abigail as she looked down with embarrassment.

"There's no need to be sorry. I know what you meant. I will say I'm happy to be home and to see you. I was wondering if we could dine out tonight for our date. There's a place I would like to take you, and we need to be seen in public together...for the publicity."

"That sounds great! When would you like to leave?"

"I was thinking around seven."

"I'll be ready," she said as she stood up and put away her calendar.

At seven o'clock sharp, there was a knock on their joining door. Princess Abigail opened it. Prince Everett was standing there dressed up. When he saw her, his eyes lit up. "Oh! You look beautiful!"

She was putting on her black gloves. "Thank you. You look nice yourself."

"Shall we go?" asked the prince as he held out his arm.

She grabbed her handbag and took hold of his arm, and they walked out the door together. "How do you like your new room?" asked Princess Abigail as they were walking down the stairs.

"I'll adjust. I will say, I really like my suite mate," he said with a smile. "What about you? How do you like your new room?"

"It will all depend on whether you snore or not." They laughed.

The chauffeur walked over to open the door for Princess Abigail. Prince Everett held up his hand for him to stop. "I've got it," said the prince as he insisted on opening the door for Princess Abigail.

"Oh, a prince and a gentleman. Aren't you the entire package?" said Princess Abigail with playful sarcasm when the prince got into the car.

"I do my best. After all, we are still technically in the honeymoon stage." She laughed.

When they arrived at the restaurant, they literally received the royal treatment. Reporters were everywhere. There were flashing lights in every direction. Once again the prince insisted on helping Princess Abigail. He took her hand and helped her out of the car. When they entered the restaurant, they were seated right away near the entrance for publicity for the restaurant.

As they were waiting for their first course, Princess Abigail noticed a couple who walked in. It was obvious they weren't of the upper class. The hostess rudely exclaimed, "You will have to leave and come back another time. We have our Royal Highnesses dining with us tonight. We need to make a good impression. We are sorry, but we don't have any tables available for you. You should try somewhere else, perhaps on the other side of town."

Princess Abigail looked around the restaurant. There were several open tables.

"We can pay our way. Please, it's our wedding anniversary."

"You need to leave at once. Like I said, we don't have a table for you. We only have room for—"

The man stopped her. "We know. The rich." The couple turned around to leave.

Princess Abigail stood up, tossed her napkin onto the table, and walked over to where the hostess and the couple were standing. Prince Everett stood up and followed her, unaware of what was going on. "If your restaurant is too good for these nice people, then it's too good for us also," said Princess Abigail. She turned to the couple. "Happy anniversary!"

With huge smiles on their faces, he bowed, and she curtsied. "Thank you, Your Highness."

Princess Abigail walked out of the restaurant, furious. Prince Everett wasn't sure what had happened, but he followed her. While they waited for the car, Princess Abigail was quiet at first. When they were on their way back to the palace, she opened up. "My mother—whom I never got to meet because she died during childbirth—wasn't from an upper-class family. She was a nurse. My papa, who was from an upper-class family, was badly injured after being thrown off a horse. He was in the hospital for several weeks. She took good care of him. They fell in love and married. They were married three wonderful years before I was born, and she died. My papa was adamant about teaching me humility, and even though we were considered upper class, we weren't better than anyone.

"My dad never remarried, even though he had many prospects. It makes me angry when people are treated badly because of their class. We don't get to choose the families into which we are born. So why should people look down on others for something they can't help?" She sighed and looked into the prince's eyes. "With all that being said, when looking for a wife, don't limit yourself to love someone only from a certain class. You could really miss out."

The prince admired her conviction and how she stood up for what she thought was right. "Thank you for sharing this with me. I understand why you would be upset."

Trying to lighten the mood, the prince changed the subject. "Well, we definitely made our public appearance. I guess we will read about it tomorrow in the newspaper." They laughed. "As of yet, I have a bad track record with planning our dates. Maybe you should plan the next one."

She giggled. "I can't say I've made it easy on you. I'm surprised you still want to be around me."

"There's nothing you could ever do to make me not want to be around you." She blushed. "Well, since this didn't work out, is there anything else you would like to do tonight?" asked the prince. "My evening is free."

Princess Abigail thought about it for a second. "How about we go around the palace and meet as many of the servants that we can and thank them for their service to us?"

He looked at her as if she had lost her mind. "Are you serious? Is that really what you want to do on a Friday night?"

"Absolutely! The servants are treated like they are invisible. We bark out our demands and orders, and they do everything we ask. They rarely hear a thank-you from us. They are people like you and me. They have feelings, lives, and dreams. Yes, they get paid for their service, but I feel they should also be appreciated. These are the people who make the food you eat and know many of your secrets. If you treat them well, they will give you their loyalty."

The prince rubbed his chin while thinking it over, "You do make a strong argument. All right. Let's do it! Where should we start?"

"How about we start with our generous chauffeur, who has been standing outside, waiting for us for the past twenty minutes to exit the car? After that, we should go to the kitchen since we haven't had dinner yet," she said with light sarcasm.

The prince made a gesture, and the chauffeur opened the prince's car door. After he got out, he helped Princess Abigail out of the car. Before they walked off, the prince held out his hand and shook the chauffeur's hand. "Thank you for your service to us. You are good at your job and very much appreciated!"

The chauffeur was very surprised. He bowed. "Thank you, Your Highness. It is my pleasure to serve you." The chauffeur got into the car to park it with a huge smile on his face.

"Did you see how his face lit up over a few simple words and seconds of your time? You just made his day," said Princess Abigail as they walked into the palace. Next, they walked into the kitchen. It was very busy and chaotic. When the servants saw them, they stopped what they were doing. One could have heard a pin drop. The men bowed, and the women curtsied. "Your Royal Highnesses," they all said in unison.

"The prince and I are here to say thank you for all you do for all of us. For the wonderful food and service you provide every day. You are greatly appreciated!" said Princess Abigail as she walked around the room, shaking hands. The servants all were smiling. It was like sunshine entering a dreary room.

The prince marveled at Abigail while she was speaking to the people. She was the most genuine person he had ever known. "We don't want to keep you any longer. We know you are very busy. You may go back to your work." Princess Abigail walked over to one of the kitchen maids. "Do you mind sending up two dinners for the prince and me in about an hour? Our dinner plans changed at the last minute. I'm sure you'll read all about it in tomorrow's newspaper."

"Yes, Your Highness," she said with a curtsy.

"Thank you." Princess Abigail and Prince Everett left the kitchen and went to the laundry room. When the servants saw them, they stopped what they were doing. They were very surprised to see them! They looked as though they had seen a ghost. Princess Abigail looked at the prince. "It's your turn to say something."

For the first time in his life, he looked into the servants' eyes and saw them as people like him. "We are here to say thank you for all that you do for us. You are very important and valued. It's people like you who keep this place going. We won't keep you any longer from your work. We just wanted to express our appreciation."

Their faces expressed complete joy. "Thank you, Your Highness," they said. After Everett saw the people's reactions, he wondered why he had never done anything like this before.

It was so easy to brighten someone else's day. He felt as though he were receiving more joy from the experience than he was able to give. They went around the palace, shaking hands and thanking all the servants they could find.

After about an hour, they went back to their rooms for dinner. When they walked into their separate rooms, they each found a dinner plate on their table. Prince Everett knocked on Princess Abigail's door. "Would you like to come to my room and at least eat together on our date night?"

She smiled. "Sure," she said as she picked up her plate and brought it into the prince's room. As Prince Everett was putting a bite into his mouth, Princess Abigail grabbed his hand, bowed her head, and said, "Thank you, Lord, for this enjoyable evening. Thank you for all of the wonderful people who keep this place going. Help us never to forget that you love us all the same, and we are to love like you do. Thank you for this food and your provision. In Jesus's name, I pray. Amen."

"I must say, I really enjoyed myself tonight. I have been guilty of looking right through the servants and forgetting they are people just like me. Tonight was the first time I've ever been to the laundry room and kitchen."

"The important thing is to keep remembering to do this from here on out."

The prince smiled. "I'm sure you will keep reminding me."

"You're right about that." They both laughed. They continued to laugh and talk and finished their dinner.

While the prince was talking, Princess Abigail realized that she hadn't enjoyed anyone's company so much since Luke had died. She looked at the clock. "Oh my goodness! We've been talking for almost two hours! I guess we should be getting to bed. I'm sorry to have kept you for so long."

"Please don't apologize. I have really enjoyed talking to you and getting to know you more." He gazed into her eyes and continued, "You can have as much of my time as you please."

Princess Abigail stood up abruptly, and the prince stood as well. He walked her to her room. He took her hand and kissed it. "Thank you for such a wonderful evening. I'm already looking forward to next Friday."

Abigail blushed. "Thank you," she said with a smile as she closed the door behind her.

Prince Everett and Andrew were at a party. Andrew noticed the prince retreating and staying off to himself. He walked over to him. "What's wrong with you? You've barely spoken to anyone tonight. There are so many beautiful eligible women here who would love to get to know you."

The prince put down his drink. "These parties are becoming dull and redundant. I'm rather tired of them. I honestly would enjoy myself more if I were at the palace."

"Oh, I'm sure you would. Abigail is turning you into an old man."

"Leave her out of this. It has nothing to do with her. It's time for me to grow up."

"You are right! It's time for you to find a wife...and I know just the girl. I insist that you and Abigail come to my place this weekend. I will invite Lady Vanessa. I think she is a good match for you. I met her a few nights ago at dinner with some friends." The prince was reluctant, but he agreed for them to come.

Abigail walked into the orphanage with a huge smile on her face. As always, she loved being around the children and helping out however she could. Sometimes she would go in the mornings to help with the children's schooling and chores. At other times she would come in the evenings to help with dishes and putting children to bed. It was very hard for the staff to let Princess Abigail do things like the laundry, cleaning, and dishes, even though she had insisted on doing them. She left her title at the door. To them she was just Abigail—a volunteer to help wherever she was needed.

The staff and the children absolutely adored her. Her presence was a breath of fresh air. She was loving and encouraging to everyone. When Ruby saw her, she ran to Princess Abigail. "I missed you so much!"

"I missed you too, precious. How was your weekend?"

"It was good. It would have been better if you were here.

Can you live here with us? I never want you to leave," said Ruby as she hugged Princess Abigail's leg.

"Aww," said Princess Abigail as she knelt down to be eye to eye with her. "I would love to live here with you. This is my favorite place to visit. I just can't live here. I have to do my duties as a princess. I promise you that I will come here as much as I possibly can. If you ever need me, I will always try my best to be here for you."

"I love you, Abigail," said Ruby as she gave her a hug and kissed her on her cheek.

"I love you, too, Ruby."

Other children joined in, hugging and surrounding Princess Abigail. "Let's go outside and play," said Princess Abigail. They followed her outside. They played tag and hide-and-seek. They had a wonderful time. She kept them busy while the staff had their monthly planning meeting. It was her favorite day of the month because they mostly played.

At the end of the day, as Princess Abigail walked into the palace, the prince was walking out. She was beaming with joy.

"You look like you had a good day! Let me guess—you've been at the orphanage."

"You guessed right," she said.

"Andrew has invited us to stay this weekend at his estate. That will count as our date for this week. Are you in agreement with that?" asked the prince.

"Are you sure he wants me to come too? He knows about our arrangement."

"Oh no. He insisted that you come too. He has a beautiful garden he wants to show you."

She thought about it for a second. "In that case I'll come. I don't want to be rude."

Chapter Nine

On the way to Lord Macentire's estate, Abigail was enjoying the drive and the scenery. She noticed the prince was being exceptionally quiet and acted like he was troubled. "Is something wrong? You seem quiet today."

"Andrew has invited a lady to join us for the weekend. He thinks we might be a good match. He has told her about the nature of our relationship."

Princess Abigail felt instantly sick to her stomach. She tried to keep her composure and pretend that it didn't bother her. "Are you nervous?"

"Maybe a little. It's hard to know if someone likes me for me or because I'm a prince. Most women aren't like you," replied Prince Everett with a shrug.

"I really shouldn't be coming along. I will only be in the way."

"That isn't true," rebutted the prince.

She thought things over for a few minutes. "Now it makes sense. I was invited to keep Andrew company for the weekend." She looked out the window to keep from showing her feelings of aggravation.

"I want you to be there. Your opinion means a lot to me," said the prince as he put his hand on hers.

Princess Abigail moved her hand. "I'm telling you in advance: I'm completely staying out of this. I won't let my opinion influence you in any way. This is a decision that you need to make on your own."

The prince looked into her eyes with amazement. "You are the first person in my entire life to say something like that to me. Everyone always wants to tell me what I should or shouldn't do or give their opinion."

Princess Abigail took a deep breath, "Did you know she was coming before you asked me to come?"

He hesitated, "Yes. I really wanted you to be there, and I knew you wouldn't if you knew about it. It's not only me. Andrew wants you there also."

She sighed. "I guarantee she won't. This really isn't fair for her either. Please promise me that you will never do anything like this again."

"I promise," said Prince Everett.

They were quiet for the rest of the way. Princess Abigail was questioning herself about why she felt so hurt and sad. Why was this bothering her so much? She knew this day would come, that one day he would fall in love with someone, and she would go back to the life she had before. She knew it would be better if it happened sooner rather than later, she thought. The longer things continued to go on, the more settled into her life she would become, and the more it would hurt when she had to move on. She knew she needed him to find love quickly. She would do her best to help make that happen.

When Prince Everett and Princess Abigail arrived, Andrew and Lady Vanessa walked out with the servants to greet them. After the prince helped Princess Abigail out of the car, Andrew bowed, and Lady Vanessa curtsied. "Your Highnesses."

Andrew took Princess Abigail's hand and kissed it. "I'm glad you were able to come."

Princess Abigail smiled. "Thank you for inviting me."

"Let me introduce you both to Lady Vanessa."

"It's nice to meet you, milady," said Everett.

"The pleasure is all mine," said Lady Vanessa in an alluring voice. She was very beautiful, Princess Abigail thought. She had dark hair and was tall and slender. Her dark-brown eyes looked at the prince as if she wanted to eat him for dinner.

"Shall we go inside, everyone?" asked Andrew as he motioned towards the doors. "I'll give you a tour of the place," he continued as he led the way, and they followed. It was very grand and beautiful. Prestigious artwork covered each wall.

After the tour everyone sat down in the drawing room for tea. "Let's all take a couple of hours to rest and change for dinner," said Andrew as he lounged back in a chair.

"I noticed you didn't bring a lady's maid, Princess Abigail. Would you like to borrow mine to help you dress for dinner?" asked Vanessa sarcastically.

"I gave my maid the weekend off. I'm perfectly capable of dressing myself, but thank you for your kind offer," she responded with poise.

Everyone went to their separate rooms. Abigail felt completely out of place. She wished she had never come. It was too late now. She was there. The only thing to do was to make the most of it. They were planning a picnic tomorrow in the gardens. She knew she would enjoy that.

As Princess Abigail was dressing for dinner, she thought about how much she was going to miss the children at the orphanage when the prince married, especially little Ruby. She also had been enjoying Everett's friendship. It didn't seem right for things to carry on as they had. Their dates needed to be strictly business from now on.

She looked at the clock. It was time for everyone to go downstairs. She took her time and was the last one down. Everyone but Princess Abigail had cocktails before dinner. Prince Everett noticed Abigail retreating. He wanted to be near her, but Lady Vanessa wouldn't leave his side for a minute. She was constantly beside him, and they were getting along well.

"Are you alright, Abigail? You seem quiet," asked Andrew as he put his hand on her shoulder.

"I'm fine. I'm just tired. Before I left to come here today,

I folded seven loads of laundry. I made twelve beds and played several rounds of tag with twelve children."

Overhearing what Princess Abigail had said, Vanessa interrupted. "Did you say that you folded laundry and made beds?"

Princess Abigail smiled mischievously. "That's just some of the many jobs you do as the princess of Noreland. It's hard work."

Lady Vanessa looked at the prince in disbelief. Prince Everett looked at Princess Abigail and laughed.

"I volunteer three days a week at the local orphanage. I gladly do laundry, make beds, wipe messy noses, and help out however I can."

"But you're a princess!"

"God didn't put me here to just take up space, wave, and look pretty."

"Well, I'm proud to say that I've never folded laundry or made a bed in my life," said Lady Vanessa with a smirk on her face.

"And why would you be proud to say that? What makes you better than the people who make your bed and do your laundry? What if you lost your fortune and you were left with nothing? Could you even dress yourself, prepare food, or even survive?" asked Princess Abigail.

"Well, that's never going to happen!" responded Lady Vanessa as she looked at her nails.

"For your sake, let's hope not," responded Princess

Abigail with disgust. The prince looked at Princess Abigail with absolute amusement.

The butler walked in. "Dinner is served."

"Perfect timing!" said Andrew as he wedged in between the two women.

Princess Abigail was seated by Andrew, and the prince was seated by Lady Vanessa. "You look very beautiful this evening, Abigail."

"Thank you," she said with a smile as she looked down at her food.

"What do you think of the place?"

"It's very beautiful! I'm really looking forward to seeing the gardens tomorrow."

"I'm really looking forward to showing them to you," responded Andrew flirtatiously.

"If you don't mind me asking, Andrew, why haven't you chosen to marry?"

"Are you asking?" They both laughed.

"I'm just curious. Most people our age seem to think it's their sole purpose in life."

He shrugged. "I just haven't found anyone I want to spend the rest of my life with. Most of the women I meet are beautiful, but they lack excitement and depth. They are only interested in their social calendars."

Princess Abigail laughed, which caught Everett's attention. He loved her laugh. Lady Vanessa quickly drew his attention back to her.

"That's why you need to look beyond the upper class," said Princess Abigail.

"Aren't you a contradiction? You are from the upper class."

"Yes, and I loathe their company. There is so much more to life than dresses, balls, and what other people think about you. That's another reason I love going to the orphanage. Those children don't care if I'm rich or poor. Beautiful or ugly. They love me for me. That's how I want to be loved and to love others."

"Ah, Abigail, you truly are an amazing woman!"

"I'm really not. I just have different values than most of the people you choose to be around."

"Well, you are definitely different from anyone I've ever met." He brushed her hair back from her face.

She pulled back as though she felt uncomfortable. "I'm really tired. Thank you for a delightful evening. Please excuse me." She stood up; so did everyone else. She walked out of the dining room and toward the stairs.

Prince Everett followed her. "Abigail." She turned around. "Is everything all right?" he asked with concern.

"Everything is fine. I'm just tired." They stood there a moment, looking at each other awkwardly. "You shouldn't keep her waiting. I'll see you in the morning."

"Good night," responded the prince as he watched her walk up the stairs.

Lillian was back at the palace, sitting at the servants' table and reading a book. The servants were even more jealous of her for the fact that Princess Abigail had given her the entire weekend off. Archie had a few free minutes, so he sat down next to her. "Are you enjoying your book?"

Lillian looked up with delight to see Archie. "Who doesn't enjoy a good love story?" he said with sarcasm.

"Well, if you don't have it yourself, at least you can read about it," said Lillian.

"I'm sure you have lads lining up to court you."

"Ha ha, you don't have to be mean," responded Lillian as she closed her book and considered getting up to leave.

"What do you mean? A girl as pretty as you...I thought for sure you had a beau."

Lillian blushed. "Well, you thought wrong."

"So does that mean you're free for tonight?"

"Free as a bird."

"Can I take you to dinner when I'm off work?"

"I would like that," responded Lillian, trying not to show her giddiness.

"All right. It's a date. Be ready around seven thirty," he said as he got up to go back to work.

Lillian couldn't stop smiling. She got up from the table and went straight to her room to pick out something to wear. She had never been on a date before. She only had a few choices, but she stewed it over until she decided. She wished

Princess Abigail were there to ask her opinion and to get some advice.

―――

The next morning Princess Abigail walked into the dining room refreshed. Everyone stood up. Lady Vanessa and Andrew curtsied and bowed.

"Did you sleep well?" asked Andrew as he pulled her chair out.

"I did. Thank you for asking," she said as she sat down and put her napkin in her lap. "How late did you all stay up?"

"I went to bed soon after you. I'm not sure about these lovebirds," said Andrew with a mischievous smile. The prince glared at Andrew. Princess Abigail held back her feelings of disappointment and smiled at the prince.

Andrew leaned over and whispered into Princess Abigail's ear, "I'm sorry if I made you feel uncomfortable last night at dinner when I touched your hair. I am an affectionate person, and I would never want to overstep my bounds."

Princess Abigail wiped her mouth before she responded, "Your affection only makes me feel uncomfortable because I'm not ready to reciprocate that affection. Honestly I'm not sure if or when I will ever be able to."

Andrew took her hand and looked deeply into her eyes. "I appreciate your honesty, and I feel you're worth the wait, even if it means nothing will ever come out of it."

She smiled genuinely. "Thank you." Prince Everett watched their exchange of words and couldn't deny his jealousy.

They all finished breakfast and went outside to walk the gardens. Andrew held out his arm for Princess Abigail to hold onto. She took it. Prince Everett offered his arm to Lady Vanessa. They walked through the gardens. Princess Abigail's face beamed with joy while looking at all of the beautiful flowers and sculptures. She loved gardens and being outside. It was such a beautiful day. The sun was shining, and the weather was perfect.

"I know it's not the palace, but could you see yourself living here?" asked Andrew as he searched her face.

Princess Abigail looked at him, puzzled.

"I think you are the most amazing woman I have ever met. You are the kind of woman I could see myself spending the rest of my life with. Eventually Everett is going to find love, and your arrangement will be off. And what about you? Don't you deserve love and happiness? I can offer you that."

Princess Abigail was caught off guard, especially after the conversation they'd had at breakfast. "You have a lot to offer a lady. You're charming, handsome; you have the means. In regard to me, however, you barely know me. Once you get to know me more, you may not feel the same. I'm known to have a sharp tongue, and I can be overly passionate at times. Although I am very flattered by your offer, as I mentioned before, I'm not ready to love again, and I don't know if I ever will be."

He shrugged. "I guess I feel as though I know you more than I actually do due to Everett always talking about you."

"I hope it's all good things," she said with a laugh.

"Oh, every word." He stopped walking for a second and continued, "I just hope that you will give us the opportunity to get to know each other better. Who knows? Perhaps you may change your mind. I'll never rush you, but I hope you will think about my offer and keep it in the back of your mind."

Andrew could see that she was starting to feel uncomfortable, so he wanted to lighten the mood. He leaned over and whispered in her ear, "I know you like to play kid games, so...*tag!* You're it!" He tagged her shoulder and ran.

She ran after him with a huge smile on her face. After dodging a few bushes, she tagged him, and he ran after her. They played for a few minutes, tagging each other back and forth.

Everett envied their playful interaction. He had never seen Abigail's playful side. Lady Vanessa stood up and tagged Everett, and he chased after her. Then they all joined in playing together. They were all laughing and playing like kids. The servants brought out a blanket and food for the picnic while they were playing.

Out of breath, they all walked over to the blanket and sat down to eat. Andrew sat down beside Princess Abigail and Lady Vanessa next to Everett. Prince Everett saw how Andrew looked at Princess Abigail. He couldn't blame him, but it did bother him greatly.

"I've heard that you like dancing, Abigail. Would you like for us all to dance tonight?" asked Andrew as he handed her a flower he had picked.

"I would like that!" she said with excitement.

"So would I," said Lady Vanessa as she looked at Everett with a flirtatious smile.

After they had eaten and had sat there awhile, they decided to walk back inside to rest and change for dinner. A servant ran out and stopped Andrew. He handed him a piece of paper. Andrew told the others to go on as he stopped to read it and met up with the group before they went upstairs. "I hate to inform you all, but we have a small change of plans. We will still have dinner and dancing; however, Lord and Lady Jillian will be joining us tonight. They found out that our Royal Highnesses are here, and they have basically invited themselves here for the evening. They don't know about our precarious arrangement, so we will have to keep the appearance of the prince and princess being an actual couple and abide by the formalities."

Lady Vanessa was very upset, and it showed on the look on her face. Princess Abigail held back a smile, trying not to upset Lady Vanessa any more than she already was. They all went upstairs to change for dinner.

Everyone but the prince and princess were downstairs waiting for dinner. Everett waited at Abigail's door in order for them to go down together. When she walked out, he looked her up and down. "You look beautiful!"

"Thank you. You look handsome." He held out his arm, and she grabbed it. He had missed her touch. He enjoyed the short amount of time he had her all to himself.

When they walked down the stairs, the men bowed, and the women curtsied. "Your Royal Highnesses," they said. Everyone walked into the dining room. When they sat down, Lady Vanessa somehow managed to sit by the prince.

"I'm embarrassed to admit it, but when we found out that your Royal Highnesses were here, we kind of invited ourselves," said Lord Jillian in his robust voice as he put food on his plate.

"You know you are always welcome here," said Lord Macentire.

"You are such a beautiful couple. You're even more attractive in person than in your pictures," gushed Lady Jillian. Princess Abigail and Prince Everett looked at each other and smiled. Lady Vanessa rolled her eyes and sat there with her arms crossed.

"It is very nice to meet you both. We are glad you were able to come and that we were able to meet you," said Princess Abigail.

"With your reputation, Your Highness, I'm sure it wasn't easy to settle down, even with someone as lovely as Princess Abigail. How do you like married life?" asked Lord Jillian as he took a bite.

Ignoring Lord Jillian's rudeness, the prince looked into Princess Abigail's eyes. "Honestly, I'm enjoying it greatly. I thought she was amazing when we first met, but the more I get to know her, the more I discover how I have no idea just how amazing she really is."

Princess Abigail blushed and gave him an affectionate smile. Lady Vanessa sighed and changed the subject. "How long have you and Lady Jillian been married?" They answered her question, but she wasn't interested in them at all. She did everything she could to keep Everett's attention on her for the rest of the meal.

After dinner everyone left the dining room. Andrew turned on some music. He walked over to Lady Vanessa, and they began to dance. Prince Everett and Princess Abigail followed and then Lord and Lady Jillian. While they were dancing, Everett made conversation. "You and Andrew seem to be getting along well."

"I'm enjoying his company. He's very charming. How do you like Lady Vanessa? She seems to really like you."

"I would say there's potential. What do you think of her?"

"She's very beautiful. Other than our little disagreement, I haven't had an actual conversation with her to even have an opinion. I know she doesn't like me."

The prince smiled. "That's all right. I like you enough for both of us."

Princess Abigail smiled and gazed into Everett's eyes and he into hers. Andrew walked over. "May I cut in?" He took Princess Abigail's hand, and they traded partners. Everyone danced and had a wonderful time.

Before Lord and Lady Jillian left, they walked over to Prince Everett and Princess Abigail. "Your Royal Highnesses, it was an honor to meet you both. I've never seen a couple more in love," said Lady Jillian.

"It was a pleasure to meet you both. Perhaps we'll meet again," responded Princess Abigail.

"We would love that."

When the couple left, Lady Vanessa walked over to Everett. "You sure played your parts well. You had them actually believing you were in love."

The prince looked over at Abigail. She was looking at one of the many paintings on the wall. "I suppose we did," he said halfheartedly.

Andrew joined Princess Abigail and began to explain the painting. He moved in closer to her and put his arm around her. Prince Everett couldn't help but notice. He pretended to be listening to Lady Vanessa as she babbled about her social calendar for next month, but his attention was on Andrew and Abigail. He couldn't help the feelings of jealousy that swelled up inside him.

Uncomfortable with their closeness, Princess Abigail slowly pulled away from Andrew. "Thank you for another wonderful evening, Andrew. I really should be getting to bed. I'll see you in the morning."

Andrew walked her to the bottom of the stairs and kissed her hand. "I'm really glad you decided to come this weekend."

"Thank you. So am I," she responded with a smile as she turned and walked up the stairs.

The next morning after breakfast, everyone walked outside to say their goodbyes before everyone went their own way. Lady Vanessa reached out and took the prince's hand. "When can I see you again? I'm free this Friday."

"I can't do Fridays. I have a weekly date with Abigail on Fridays."

She sighed with disgust. "What about Saturday instead?"

He thought about it for a second. "Saturday would be great!" He kissed her hand. "It's been a pleasure. I look forward to seeing you on Saturday."

Lady Vanessa smiled and waved flirtatiously. He got into the car.

Andrew was standing beside the car, talking to Princess Abigail. He took her hand and kissed it. "Don't forget about my offer. Just think about it." She smiled. Andrew helped her into the car, leaned over, and kissed her on the cheek. He stood up and pointed at the prince. "I will see you next Thursday for croquet. You can join us if you would like, Abigail."

"I wouldn't want to make you both look bad," she joked. They all laughed.

"Let's do this again soon," said Andrew as he closed the car door. They started to drive away.

There was silence for a while on the way back. Princess Abigail could see that the prince was thinking. He seemed a little distant toward her. "So are you going to see Lady Vanessa again?" she asked.

"This coming Saturday."

Abigail felt sick to her stomach but hid her feelings. "Oh! So soon. You must really like her. Is she someone you could imagine yourself marrying?"

"I guess we'll find out."

Princess Abigail could tell something was bothering him. She wasn't quite sure what it was.

"So what is the offer Andrew was talking to you about?"

She hesitated. "He wants me to think about marrying him after you find love and marry."

"*What!* You barely know each other! Are you actually thinking about it?"

Princess Abigail had never seen the prince like this. He was angry. "I told him I wasn't ready to think about it, and I may never be, but I'm not completely ruling it out. He told me he wouldn't push me into it; he just wants me to think about it and for us to get to know each other better. There's no harm in thinking about it," said Princess Abigail defensively.

"I thought you were never going to marry?"

"I've decided that I'm just going to continue to pray about what I should do and follow my heart—which is the same advice I would give to you."

They were silent for the rest of the trip. The prince was

furious with Andrew. How could he be flirting with his wife? He quickly caught himself in his stupidity, realizing she was only his wife legally. How could he blame him? She was truly amazing. After a few minutes, his anger subsided. When they arrived at the palace, Prince Everett opened the door for Princess Abigail and helped her out of the car. The servants came over and got their luggage. As they were walking to their rooms together, Princess Abigail said, "Thank you for bringing me along this weekend. I really enjoyed myself."

"Thank you for coming. It wouldn't have been nearly as fun if you hadn't been there."

"I guess I'll see you on Friday," said Princess Abigail as she opened the door to her room.

"This time I will plan the date. I need to redeem myself for the past two that I've blown. I refuse to be a failure."

She laughed. "I don't know if I should be worried or excited," she said as she walked into her room, and the prince went to his.

Chapter Ten

Abigail was unpacking. She heard a knock at the door. "Come in."

Lillian walked in. "I will do that for you, Your Highness." She looked as if she'd been crying.

"What's wrong, Lillian?" Lillian tried holding it in, but she broke down crying. Princess Abigail walked over, put her arms around her, and held her until she was able to speak. She was wondering whether someone had died.

Prince Everett heard crying coming from Abigail's room. He knocked on the door, and then, without an invitation, opened the door to find out what was wrong. When he opened the door, he saw Abigail's maid in her arms, weeping, as she held her and comforted her. "What's wrong?"

"I'm not sure yet," she said as she motioned for him to leave.

"Let me know if there's anything I can do." He closed the door, leaving it cracked open a little to hear what was going on.

Lillian finally calmed down enough to speak. "Friday night I went on a date with Archie. We were having a really good time. He took me to a pub because I had never been to one before or ever had alcohol, so he urged me to try it. We both ended up having too much to drink, and went back to his room, and we..." She cried even more tears. "I let things go too far, and we..." There were more tears and sobbing.

"I get it. You don't have to say anymore." Princess Abigail held her tight and let her cry. "I didn't know who else to talk to. I only have one other friend here besides Archie. I've been avoiding him since it happened."

"You know you can always talk to me about anything. I don't condone what you did, but I will never judge you."

"Thank you. I know God is so disappointed in me. I hate myself, and I know God must hate me too," she said as she wept and sobbed.

Princess Abigail lifted Lillian's face to look her in the eyes. "There is nothing you have done or ever will do to make God hate you. He has and always will love you, no matter what you do. His love is unconditional. I would dare even to say he isn't even disappointed *in* you but rather *for* you. Now that this has happened, you will have to deal with the consequences like you're experiencing them now. When we don't do things His way, it always causes misery, sadness, and confusion. The beauty of it all is, when we are genuinely sorry and repent for our sin, there's forgiveness."

Lillian wiped her face, "What if I'm with child?"

"Let's not worry about that right now, but if you are, I will be there for you."

Prince Everett stood there at the door, listening. He was blown away at Princess Abigail's compassion and her wisdom. He knew that Lady Vanessa's greatest flaw was that she wasn't Abigail.

On Friday, Abigail walked into her room to change and clean up after being at the orphanage all day. She found an invitation on her bed. She opened it. It was from the prince. She was to meet him in the garden for a picnic dinner. Excited, she walked out to the garden. Prince Everett was sitting down on a blanket with a beautiful picnic set up. "I'm impressed! You really outdid yourself."

"I was thinking about how much you love the garden and how much fun we had at the picnic last weekend...and here we are."

"How thoughtful," she said as she blushed. She sat down beside him, and they began to eat.

"How was your day?" asked the prince while he poured her a drink.

"It was wonderful, as always. Ruby asks me every day to

move into the orphanage. I guess when you marry and I'm banished from the palace, I could always go and live there." They both laughed. "Speaking of marrying, what are you planning for your date tomorrow with Lady Vanessa?"

"Because we have to keep this from the public, I thought I'd bring her here for a tour of the palace. And then maybe dinner in my room." Princess Abigail looked away to hide the fact that it bothered her.

Just then, it began to rain out of nowhere. Princess Abigail began laughing so hard she could barely breathe. "It's official! I'm not planning any more of our dates," said the prince while he sat there, getting drenched and laughing.

When they pulled themselves together, they began cleaning up and collecting the things from the picnic. When they had as much as they could carry, they stood up and began quickly walking back to the palace. Princess Abigail slipped on some mud and fell down, splattering mud all over her dress and face. Prince Everett was laughing so hard he could hardly stand up. After a couple of minutes, he held out his hand to help her up. She grabbed his hand and pulled him down to the ground also. They just sat there laughing with the rain pouring down on them.

After a few minutes, he stood and helped her up. They stood there looking into each other's eyes. He pulled her close to him. He cupped her face in his hands and slowly leaned down to kiss her. And *boom!* The sound of thunder jarred them both. "I've got to get you inside," said Everett with concern.

He picked her up in his arms and ran with her inside the palace, leaving all of the picnic stuff. After they got in, he was out of breath, and they were both drenched. "Go ahead and go up to change, so you don't catch a cold. We'll call it a night. I'll go and collect the things we left. I'm sorry it turned out like this," he said as he wiped the mud off her face.

"You have nothing to be sorry for. This is my favorite date we've ever had. I'll never forget it." She gently kissed him on the cheek and quickly walked upstairs.

The next day Princess Abigail walked in the garden like she did every Saturday morning, enjoying the beautiful flowers and statues. She couldn't stop thinking about the way the prince had looked her in the eyes and how they'd almost kissed and the way he scooped her up in his arms and ran her to safety. She was very aware that in only a few hours, he would be walking this same garden with Lady Vanessa. She refused to let herself think of it anymore. They had just gotten caught up in the moment. It meant nothing.

Later that evening, Princess Abigail was sitting on her love seat, reading a book. She took a break to rest her eyes. She walked over to her window to enjoy her view of the garden—and there stood Prince Everett and Lady Vanessa, standing quite close to each other. She watched as Lady Vanessa reached down, took the prince's hand, and pulled him in closer to herself. Lady Vanessa looked up and caught a glimpse of Abigail looking out of the window. She smiled at her as if she were trying to rub it in.

Princess Abigail quickly backed away from the window. She refused to let her evening be ruined. She thought of the orphanage and how the children were continuously asking for her to have a sleepover with them. So she wrote a little note to let Lillian know where she would be. She packed a little bag and walked out her door.

Prince Everett and Lady Vanessa had just turned the corner to the hallway to his room. He looked up and saw Princess Abigail walking farther down, carrying a bag. *Where is she going?* he thought. "Wait here," said the prince to Lady Vanessa. Then he ran down the hall, shouting, "Abigail! Abigail!"

She stopped. She turned and saw the prince running toward her. "Where are you going?" asked Prince Everett while catching his breath.

"The children are always wanting me to have a sleepover with them, so I decided at the last minute to do it tonight. Tomorrow morning, I will go to church with them."

"I'm sorry we haven't had a chance to talk about what happened last night," said the prince.

"There's nothing to talk about. Nothing happened. We just got caught up in the moment. I'm sure it will never happen again," replied Princess Abigail solemnly. They stood there awkwardly for a moment. "You shouldn't keep her waiting. I'll see you on Friday."

He gave her a half smile. Abigail turned around and went on her way, and Prince Everett walked back to Lady Vanessa. "You have feelings for her, don't you?" asked Lady Vanessa with disappointment in her voice.

The prince shrugged. "Yes. But she has made it crystal clear that she has no intentions of ever giving anyone her heart again and that she wants me to find love. Knowing this, I would completely understand if you don't want to see me anymore."

Lady Vanessa grabbed Prince Everett's hands and looked into his eyes. "There's nothing you could say to make me not want to see you anymore." She kissed his cheek, and they went into his room for dinner.

Chapter Eleven

Prince Everett sat up in bed. Yawning, he stretched and slowly got up. He looked out the window and saw Princess Abigail sitting in the garden, reading her Bible. Every morning that the weather allowed, she would read there on the bench underneath the magnolia tree. He watched her for a few minutes and got dressed. There was a knock on the door. "Come in."

The door opened. It was Archie. He bowed. "Your Royal Highness, her Royal Majesty would like an audience with you and Princess Abigail as soon as possible."

"Do you know what this is about?" asked the prince.

"No, Your Highness. I'm just the messenger. May I get you anything before I find Her Royal Highness?"

"No, I'm good, but thank you. Don't worry about Abigail. I will inform her. We will be there as soon as we can."

"Very well, Your Highness," said Archie as he bowed and left.

When Abigail looked up, she saw the prince walking toward her. Surprised, she stood up and started walking to meet him.

"The queen is requesting an audience with the two of us as soon as possible."

"Is everything all right?" asked Abigail with concern.

"I'm not sure what this is about."

As they walked to the queen's office, neither of them said anything. When they arrived, they were announced and sent in immediately. They walked in; he bowed, and she curtsied. "Your Majesty."

The queen walked over and kissed them both on each cheek. "Please have a seat," said the queen as she pointed to chairs beside her own. They stood until the queen sat down, and then they followed. They were eager to find out what this was all about. The queen just looked at them both for a second as if she were trying to study them. "Is everything good between the two of you?"

They looked at each other, confused by her question. "Yes," they both answered.

"The reason I'm asking is...there are rumors going around the palace that you, Everett, have been seen with someone other than your wife and that you, Abigail, have been spending nights at the orphanage away from your husband. I'm not going to ask if any of this is true or not, but I am going to remind you both that you are always being watched. If there are problems in your marriage, you need to work them out quickly and privately. We can't have any of this being read about in the newspapers. Another thing. You have been married now for nearly seven months, and in case you have an announcement to make, we have no heir. We desperately need an heir, and His Royal Majesty and I aren't getting any younger. We really want grandchildren."

Prince Everett and Princess Abigail looked at each other as the queen continued. "You never had a real honeymoon, so I have spoken with both of your private secretaries and informed them to clear your schedules for next week. You have three days to prepare. We are sending you away for… let's just call it a vacation. You will leave Sunday and return on Saturday. We are keeping it a secret because we don't want reporters following you, causing stress, and keeping you from…well, the obvious."

Princess Abigail blushed and awkwardly looked at the prince.

"I hate to rush you out, but I have my next meeting in five minutes." She stood, and they stood. She walked over and kissed them again, and they walked out.

"Well, that wasn't what I was expecting," said the prince with a smile.

"What are we going to do?" asked Princess Abigail with panic in her voice.

"We are going on this trip."

"I know that. I mean, about the heir and grandchildren part."

"We are going to continue on as we have been. My mother has always pressured me about most things in my life. She will get an heir when she gets an heir. It's not something you need to worry yourself with. The pressure is on me."

Princess Abigail heard what he said, but she still felt a great deal of pressure. Since it was to be kept a secret, she told no one. They decided not to meet that Friday since they would soon be spending nearly a week together.

Prince Everett and Princess Abigail barely spoke to each other the entire train ride there. When they arrived at the location on Sunday afternoon, they found two small, secluded cottages on the beach, one for the servants and one for just the two of them. The servants carried in their luggage and quickly left them alone. When they walked in, they noticed their cottage had a little kitchen area with a table, a small living room with a sofa, and a fireplace. There was one bedroom with a king-sized bed. They could see and hear the ocean from the bedroom window. When Princess Abigail saw the bedroom, she said adamantly, "This isn't going to work."

"I will sleep on the sofa," said Prince Everett as he searched and found extra linen. They didn't say much as they unpacked and changed for dinner.

That evening Prince Everett and Princess Abigail sat down for dinner. "I'm not exactly sure where we are, but I love this place," said Abigail while she was unfolding her napkin.

"I've been thinking. Since we're here, we should make the most of it. So since we're here for five days, what if you choose an activity for us to do together for two of the days, and I choose two of the days' activities, and on Friday we do our own thing? And every evening we have dinner together?" asked the prince, searching Princess Abigail's face to see if she was on board.

"I think that's a great idea! So who goes first?"

"Ladies go first."

"All right. I know exactly what I want to do tomorrow. Let's go out in a boat for a bit during the day and then, tomorrow evening, have dinner on the beach."

"I like the sound of that. I'll inform the servants to assist us with the boat," Everett replied.

To make conversation Princess Abigail asked, "So how are things going with you and Lady Vanessa?"

"They're going. She seems to really like me a great deal. In fact, she's very upset about this week and you and me being here alone together."

"I don't blame her. I would be upset too," said Princess Abigail.

"Andrew keeps bothering me about wanting to see you again. I told him you would let him know when you are ready."

Princess Abigail didn't want to talk about Andrew or Lady

Vanessa any longer. "I'm rather tired. I hope we can make the most of an awkward week," she said as she wiped her mouth and pushed her plate back.

"I don't see why we can't. What if we start the week off by sleeping on the beach tonight?" suggested Prince Everett. He stood up and held out his hand. "Come on."

She reluctantly took his hand, and they left the cottage. He led her out a little way back from the water. "This will be a perfect spot," said the prince while he began to smooth out the sand.

"You want to sleep here? On the sand, together?" asked Princess Abigail with uncertainty in her voice.

"Well, you can sleep over there," he said as he pointed, "and I can sleep here. Wouldn't it be incredible to wake up to the sunrise?"

She thought about it for a second. "All right. I'll get us some blankets."

"Allow me. It was my suggestion," said the prince as he got up and ran to the cottage. He came back with a blanket and pillow for each of them. They scooted back a little more so they wouldn't get caught in the tide during the night. They sat there, enjoying the beauty and sounds all around them but mostly each other's company. It was all very surreal. They had an entire beach to themselves.

"What are your thoughts about becoming king one day?" asked Princess Abigail as she looked out onto the ocean.

"Well, that question came out of nowhere." He sighed. "I

have a lot of mixed feelings. For me to be king would mean my father would be dead or be in some state of not being able to rule. I'm terrified to be the one who has to follow in his steps. He's a wonderful king, and our people love him greatly. What if I'm a failure and bring harm to our country? These are some of the concerns that constantly stay on my mind. I try not to think about it. That's probably why I have the reputation that I do. I like to be distracted, so I don't have to think about it—although it doesn't really seem to help. There are also things I would like to change. The monarchy, for one, is very old fashioned. I would like to modernize it a bit. There are other changes that I would like to make in order to make things better. We can discuss them at another time…things my father would never agree with."

"I'm sorry that you have such a heavy burden to carry," said Princess Abigail as she crawled closer to him and placed her hand on his shoulder.

"This is another reason why marrying the right person is vital. I need someone who can handle the pressures and be a strong pillar beside me." They sat there in silence for a few minutes. She could see that the conversation was causing the prince stress, so she quickly changed the subject. They talked for hours. After a while, as Princess Abigail was talking, she noticed no response from the prince. She looked over and saw that he had fallen asleep. She covered him up and went back over to her spot. Before she knew it, she was asleep too.

The next morning she woke up to the sun in her eyes.

She suddenly realized she was snuggled up next to the prince. She quickly got over to her spot. They had slept through the sunrise. After a few minutes, she woke him up. "Everett... Everett," said Princess Abigail as she gently nudged him.

"Yes," said Prince Everett, squinting his eyes in the blinding sunlight.

"We missed the sunrise."

"Well, I guess that means we'll have to do it another time."

"Perhaps. I'm going to get cleaned up for our activity," she said as she began walking back to the cottage. "I'll meet up with you at breakfast."

He sat there for a while, enjoying the incredible view and the much-needed privacy.

Prince Everett took Princess Abigail's hand to help her into the boat. They both sat down while a professional manned it. "What a perfect day to be on the water," said the prince while kicking back with a drink in his hand.

"I agree," responded Abigail as she sat down beside him. They didn't venture out too far but stayed close to the shore due to the choppy water. "The ocean is my favorite place to be. It reminds me of God. It's so powerful and mysterious yet peaceful and beautiful. It can be terrifying and yet calming. If I could live anywhere I wanted, I would have an ocean view," said Princess Abigail with her eyes glued on the water.

"Well said. I've never thought about it like that before."

They just sat back and enjoyed the ride. They had a wonderful time. They saw dolphins and different kinds of fish. After they had been out for a couple of hours, they docked the boat. When Princess Abigail was getting out of the boat, due to the rocking of the water, she fell back into Prince Everett, and he caught her. "Thank you for being there," she said with a laugh.

"My pleasure," responded the prince as he brushed her hair out of her eyes and gazed into them. He slowly released his embrace.

As they walked back to the cottage, they talked about some of the things they had seen and how much fun they'd had that day. When they arrived, the prince's private secretary was there, waiting for him to go over a few things. "I guess this means I will see you tonight at dinner," said Prince Everett as he walked toward his secretary. Princess Abigail went inside to rest for a while. After a late night and a busy day, she was tired.

That night for dinner, the servants set up a beautiful table right next to the water. It was very romantic. They had candles and rose petals on the table and all around the beach for ambiance. As they were walking down to the beach for dinner, their hands kept brushing against each other. They both fought the urge to hold the other's hand. Princess Abigail gasped with joy when she saw where they would be dining. "Oh! It's so beautiful! They really are pushing for an heir," she joked with a laugh as they both sat down for dinner.

The servants brought out the first course of the meal. Prince Everett couldn't stop staring at Princess Abigail. He enjoyed her beauty but her company even more. She was funny and fun to be with. She was refreshing—different in all the right ways from every woman he had ever known. Princess Abigail couldn't deny that things were changing between the two of them. She wasn't sure what to do about it.

Trying to start a conversation, the prince asked, "Looking back, would you say for certain that the love you shared with Luke was true love?"

She shrugged. "It had the potential to be but never had the opportunity to be."

The prince looked at her, puzzled. Had she not understood his question?

She could see his confusion. "I believe in the beginning of a relationship—that when you feel those feelings that resemble love—they are just the seeds of love. True love comes after years of taking care of each other. It requires being there for each other, in both the good times and in the bad, and sticking it out, even when it's hard and you're not at your best."

Prince Everett smiled at her. "I've had some of the best teachers and tutors in the country, yet you always seem to enlighten me, Abigail."

"Thank you!" she exclaimed as she blushed and looked away.

After dinner, Everett wiped his mouth and put down his

napkin. He stood up, walked around the table to Princess Abigail, and held out his hand. "Can I have this dance?"

She smiled in amusement. "There's no music."

"Sure there is. Listen." The waves and the water were loud and soothing. She took his hand, and they began to dance. He held her so close. She could feel his breath on her neck and also his heart racing. She enjoyed the feeling of his embrace. She was so attracted to him, and she loved the way he looked at her. She desperately wanted for him to kiss her, and she could tell he wanted to. She lifted her chin to make the first move, and then the guilt set in. She stopped herself. She thought about Lady Vanessa and how unfair this was to her. And how the prince seemed to be fond of her too.

She pulled back from him. "Thank you for the dance and for a wonderful day. If you wouldn't mind, I would like to be by myself for a bit."

Disappointed and confused about what had changed, the prince hesitated for a moment. "Very well. I'll leave you." He slowly walked back to the cottage. He looked back at her. She was sitting in the sand, holding her knees pressed up against her chest and staring at the ocean. He could tell that she was struggling with something; he hoped it was her feelings toward him.

The next morning Prince Everett was sitting at the table for breakfast. Princess Abigail sat down to join him. "Good morning. I trust you slept well?" asked the prince, ignoring the awkwardness from the night before.

"I did. I opened the window to hear the ocean, and I slept like a baby. How about you?"

"The sofa isn't bad but not really what I'm accustomed to."

"I'm so sorry. I insist that I sleep on the sofa tonight."

"Absolutely not! I will not allow it. I want you to have the bed. Besides, you need your beauty sleep."

Abigail gave him a look of aggravation. "What is that supposed to mean?"

"Isn't that what most ladies say? That they need their beauty sleep?" he said with a smirk on his face.

She smiled. "As I've heard you say before, I'm not like most ladies. So what are we going to do today?"

"We are going fishing, and we are putting a bit of a spin on it. We will have sides for the meal tonight, but the only meat that we can have is the fish that we catch today. So if we catch a lot, we will have a lot, and if we catch a little or none at all—well, that's what we'll have."

She smiled with mischief. "I like your idea. But what if, instead of it being what we catch together, we only get to eat what we have personally caught ourselves?"

"So what you're saying is...if I catch fish and you catch nothing, you will be getting zero fish tonight?"

"Something like that," said Princess Abigail with a playful smile. He stuck out his hand, and they shook on it.

When they arrived at their fishing spot, they each set up

their little area. They put their bait on their hooks. At first Prince Everett was expecting Princess Abigail to be squeamish about the worm, but then he remembered that she had been a nurse during the war and could handle more than he could. He cast his line into the water. Princess Abigail worked at it and couldn't quite do it right. Prince Everett walked over to her. "Here, let me help." He got behind her and put his arms and hands on hers to demonstrate the motion. He stepped back and let her try it on her own. She brought her arm back and cast her line in beautifully, just like he had shown her. "You may be a natural," said the prince as he walked back to his spot.

"I guess we'll see. Now what do we do?"

"We sit here and wait. Is this your first time fishing?"

"No. My dad took me a few times when I was just a girl. It's been a very long time. Do you fish often?"

"Usually when I have a lot on my mind and I need time to clear my head and think," responded the prince. "I guess I should have chosen something more fun for us to do."

"No, this is fine. I love being outside, and I enjoy your company."

They admired the view, listening to the birds and the ocean for a while. "Can I ask you a question about your faith?" asked the prince.

"You can ask. I'm not sure if I have a good answer."

"I believe in God. I go to church and have knowledge about him. I also try to live a decent life. But after being around you, I know that something is definitely missing in my 'faith' or the lack thereof. I don't have what you have, and I'm curious as to why."

Princess Abigail thought about it for a second and then gave her best answer. "Before I met you, because you are the prince, I knew who you were and where you lived and many different facts about you, things that you had made known about yourself through your actions or what others who actually knew you had shared about you. However, you and I never had a personal relationship. I only knew about you, but I didn't actually know you. Now that we actually set aside time and hang out together, I feel that we actually know each other pretty well."

The prince thought about what she said for a few minutes. "That does make a lot of sense." Just then a fish began biting on Princess Abigail's line. She got very excited. Prince Everett helped her pull it in. "Goodness! This is a good-sized fish!"

"I know who is having fish tonight!" exclaimed Princess Abigail with a playful smile. They stayed out for another hour, but Princess Abigail's fish was the only one for dinner.

During dinner the servants brought out the sides along with Princess Abigail's fish. It was cooked to perfection. She took a bite. Very dramatically she said, "This fish is wonderful. It's probably the best fish I've ever had. I really wish we could share this moment together. I bet you wish we had stuck to your original plan." They both laughed. After she took a few more jabs and had a little more fun, she cut the fish in two and gave half to the prince.

"No, I can't take it. You won fair and square; we shook on it," responded Everett as he tried to give it back.

"I couldn't have caught it if you hadn't helped me. Please, I do want to share this with you."

He reluctantly took the fish. "Ah! This is really good. Thank you for sharing this with me."

"It is my pleasure."

After dinner they walked the beach and talked. They enjoyed spending time together. The ocean view was breathtaking, but the prince couldn't keep his eyes off Princess Abigail. He desperately wanted to tell her how he was in love with her. He was afraid if he did, it would cause her to pull away from him. He couldn't take that chance.

The next morning after breakfast, Prince Everett wiped his mouth and pushed his plate back. "What's our activity for the day?"

Princess Abigail grabbed something from a drawer and tossed it to him. He shook it out and held it up. "What's this? An apron?"

"We are going to do a little baking. When it's done we can walk down to the beach and indulge."

"I hope you know what you are doing because I have never baked or cooked anything my entire life."

"I have a lot of experience. I used to bake things for people in the village all of the time," she responded.

"So what are we making?"

"Banana bread and apple pie."

"Do we have everything we need?"

"Yes. I gave Ms. Morgan a list last night of everything we would need. She brought it over first thing this morning. So put your apron on and wash your hands, and let's get started," she said with a smile but with urgency.

"Yes, ma'am!" said the prince as he began doing what she said to do. "How do I look?" he asked as he turned around and modeled the apron.

"Let's hope you bake as good as you look," said Princess Abigail with a flirtatious smile. She started getting out bowls and measuring cups and began measuring ingredients. "Can you please put two cups of flour into this bowl?" She held up a bowl, and then she held up a bag of flour. "This is flour." She gave him more simple directions, and she did other things.

The kitchen area was very small. They kept brushing against each other. The chemistry was strong between them. They both felt it. It was getting harder and harder to hold back their feelings for each other.

After the pie and banana bread were in the oven, Prince Everett asked, "So what do we do now?"

"We wait. What would you like to do while we wait?" asked Princess Abigail.

"Now that's a loaded question." He slowly walked up to her and got very close. He took the flour that was left on his hand and wiped it on her cheek with a mischievous smile. "This is flour," he said mockingly.

Princess Abigail gasped with a playful smile. She quickly grabbed some flour and rubbed it in his hair. They went back and forth with each other. They were laughing and having fun. Prince Everett pulled Abigail in his arms and looked into her eyes. He kissed her cheek gently and then her other cheek. He was going for her lips—and there was a knock at the door. He stopped and looked at her for a second. "Come in," he said in a frustrated tone.

Brian, his private secretary, opened the door. He bowed, "Your Highnesses." He saw them and the big mess. "What happened here?" he asked with a smile.

"We were just having a little fun," responded Princess Abigail.

"I'm sorry to bother you, but something has come up. Can I have a moment of your time?"

"Please excuse me, Abigail. I hope we can pick up where we left off?" responded Everett. He and Brian walked out of the cottage onto the porch.

Princess Abigail cleaned up the cottage. She didn't want the servants to have to clean up their mess. She took the desserts out of the oven and put them on the table to cool. She went into her room and cleaned herself up while smiling as she wiped the flour off her face. The window in her bedroom was partially open to so she could enjoy the cool ocean breeze. She could faintly hear the conversation between Everett and

Brian. Brian was bringing him news of the rapid spread of the Spanish flu throughout the country.

When Prince Everett came back into the cottage, he noticed that it was cleaned up and the pie and bread were on the table. They smelled and looked wonderful. He left the cabin and walked down to the beach to rinse off the flour in his hair. Princess Abigail watched him from the bedroom window. He was very handsome. She was saddened by the thought that after this week, life would go back to normal, and he would be spending all his free time with Lady Vanessa. What a wonderful week it had been. She would always cherish these memories.

"Today is our last planned activity. What have you chosen?" asked Princess Abigail as she finished breakfast. She wiped her mouth and laid her napkin on the table.

"Hiking, so get changed. When you're ready, we'll head out." Princess Abigail quickly went to her room and changed into some suitable clothes. When she came out, she turned around and modeled her fitted pants and buttoned-up shirt. He had never seen her in pants before. She asked, "How do I look?"

"You could wear a potato sack, Abigail, and still look beautiful to me." She smiled. They loaded up into the car.

The chauffeur drove them out a few miles and let them

out to go hiking. "I'll be waiting for you here when you get back, Your Highnesses."

"Thank you," they both responded. He took out a book and made himself comfortable. They set off.

"I'm following you, so I hope you know where you are going. I'm terrible with directions," said Princess Abigail.

"You're in good hands." They walked along a path, stopping to look at bugs and different types of flowers and plants. Sometimes they would just stop and sit down, get some water, and rest for a few minutes. Then they would get up and keep going. Prince Everett was surprised that Princess Abigail never complained once or asked to go back.

After a couple of hours, they came to a little creek with large rocks forming a bridge to the other side of the creek. "Let's cross over on these rocks to stay dry and go back to the path on the other side."

"Like I said, I'm following you."

He climbed up onto the first rock and then onto the second. Princess Abigail followed suit. As he was climbing over to the third rock, which was less than halfway across, he lost his balance and fell into the creek. He was in the water from his waist down. Abigail started laughing. "So much for staying dry," she said, still laughing.

He grabbed Princess Abigail's hand and pulled her in with him. "After the rain incident, I owe you one," said the prince. They laughed, splashed each other, and played in the water. He pulled her into his embrace. He just held her. Her heart was racing as she looked into his dark-brown eyes. He slowly leaned down to kiss her.

She pulled back. "We should probably start heading back." He nodded his head, disappointed.

They treaded through the water until they reached the other side. Once they reached it, they were tired and out of breath. They sat down to rest. "I have laughed and had more fun this week than I have had in years."

"Same here," responded Princess Abigail.

"Maybe we should do this again next year," said the prince.

"I don't think your girlfriend would approve. Who knows? By next year she may even be your wife. Maybe you could bring her here. I'm sure she will love it." The prince didn't know how to respond. They sat there a few more minutes in awkward silence. "Do you know how to get back?" asked Princess Abigail.

The prince stood up. He held out his hand to help her up. "Have I ever misled you?" They looked at each other for a moment. "Let's go."

He picked up the pace on the way back. They were tired and ready to get to the cottage. After an hour of hiking back, they saw the car from a distance. They ran with relief the rest of the way to it. On the way back to the cottage, they both thought about things the other had said.

At dinner, Abigail walked out of her room and sat down at the table. "I think this week caught up with me today. I took the longest nap. I hope I will be able to sleep tonight."

"I was very tired myself. I hope you enjoyed yourself today," said Prince Everett.

"Oh, I thoroughly enjoyed it…and this entire week. It was really nice getting away. It's a little sad seeing it come to an end."

"I've enjoyed the privacy and seclusion. I wish I could have more of that. It's not something I've gotten a great deal of in my life. It's funny how people are. There are people who would love to be me. To be in the public eye, to live in a palace, and to be able to have almost anything they could ever want. Yet I would like to live a simpler life and have privacy, especially since I've known you," said the prince.

"At the end of the day, the only way to be happy is to be content and thankful for what you have and who you are," said Princess Abigail.

"Good point. And I'm very thankful that tonight, at this very moment, I'm right here with you," said the prince as he looked into Princess Abigail's eyes and kissed her hand.

After dinner they headed down to the beach. As they walked, Prince Everett reached down and took Princess Abigail's hand. He held it along the way, and she let him. Her hand was so slender and soft. It fit perfectly in his.

When they got closer to the water, they stopped and looked at the beauty of the ocean. Prince Everett looked over at Princess Abigail. The breeze from the ocean was blowing her long dark hair. He leaned over and brushed it back with his fingers. He pulled her into him and kissed her passionately. The feeling of his body against hers made her tremble. They were completely lost in each other. Then, for the first time all week, they saw the flashes of photographers. Princess Abigail pulled back. "Someone must have told them we were here."

"So much for a simpler life," said the prince with frustration. They quickly walked back to the cottage. Prince Everett, discouraged, sat down on the sofa. "I'm sorry about getting you involved in all of this."

Abigail walked over and sat down beside him. She put her hand on his shoulder. "I knew what I was getting into. I would do it all over again for you."

Prince Everett slowly turned to her and cupped her face and gently kissed her. They couldn't hold back their yearning for each other any longer. They had suppressed it for so long. They fell back onto the sofa.

Desire for him rushed through her body. With her heart racing, she conjured up every ounce of self-control and pulled herself back. "I can't do this. I'm sorry," she said as she quickly got up and went to her room, closing the door behind her.

Everett lay there on the sofa. He had to cool off. He decided to take a walk down the beach. He was beyond the point of caring whether the reporters were watching. After an hour or so, he decided to go back to the cottage and lie down. It took him a long time to go to sleep. He longed and ached for Abigail.

The next morning when the prince woke up, he noticed Princess Abigail hadn't come out yet. He walked down to the beach to see if she was there. He had breakfast—and no Abigail. After some time, there was a knock on the door. Excited, Prince

I'll See You on Friday

Everett walked to the door and opened it, expecting to see Abigail. It was Brian, who handed him a letter. "Princess Abigail wanted me to give this to you. She gave it to me before the sun came up." Prince Everett opened the letter and began to read it.

Dear Everett,
I am very sorry you are reading a letter and not hearing this straight from me. I knew there was no way I could say this in person and not change my mind. The reason I left early is because this wonderful place is all an illusion. It's meant for people to create the same feelings and reactions that we almost gave into. The reality is, when this is over, you are going back to your life with Lady Vanessa, and I will go back to mine. I'm sorry for hindering you. I should have been an encouragement to you to find true love and produce an heir. Instead I stood in your way. With this being said, I release you from the obligation of our weekly dates on Fridays.

Sincerest apologies,
Abigail

When Everett finished reading the letter, he crumbled it up and threw it onto the floor. "We are leaving as soon as possible," said the prince. He was determined to get back and tell Abigail how he truly felt about her.

Chapter Twelve

When Prince Everett returned home, he looked all over the palace for Princess Abigail. When he came back to his room, he heard a noise coming from her room. He opened their joining door and found Lillian packing Princess Abigail's bag. With panic in his voice, he asked, "What are you doing? Where's Abigail?"

Lillian was startled. When she noticed it was the prince, she curtsied. "Your Highness, Princess Abigail is at the hospital with the little orphan girl Ruby. Ruby isn't doing well. She has the Spanish flu. She and Princess Abigail have a very close bond. They have from the first time they met. Princess Abigail promised her that she would always be there for her. Now she's following through on her promise.

"Princess Abigail is wearing a mask. I'm bringing a change of clothes to the hospital. She will bathe before she returns to the palace to prevent bringing in germs. They want her to stay in her room and away from you and Their Majesties for several days to secure your safety—"

The prince interrupted, "There's no way I'm staying away from her! Thank you for the information."

Lillian smiled at his obvious love for the princess. "I'm very thankful she met you, Your Highness. I haven't seen her this happy since before..." She hesitated for a second. "Well, since before Luke died. Thank you for making her so happy. She truly deserves all the happiness this world can offer. She's been through so much, and she gives and pours into everyone selflessly."

The prince could see her genuine affection for Abigail. "The truth is, she makes me happier than anyone ever has. I'm in love with her. I'm not sure if she feels the same way about me as I do about her, and I'm worried that if I tell her how I truly feel, she will only pull away from me. I will take whatever she can give, even if that's only her friendship. After all, she deserves more than I could ever offer her."

"I've known the princess for a long time, and I can honestly say I believe she has strong feelings for you as well. Please excuse my boldness, Your Highness, but I think you should give her some time. And don't give up on her. But you should definitely tell her how you feel."

Prince Everett shrugged. "Thank you for your encouraging words and for your loyalty to the princess. I know she values your friendship and service. Well, I must go."

"Your Highness," said Lillian as she curtsied.

Prince Everett left and sent word to Lady Vanessa to meet him at the palace. He wanted to end things with her before he shared his feelings with Abigail. When Lady Vanessa arrived at the palace and saw the prince standing outside, waiting for her, she quickly got out of the car and ran to him, giving him a huge hug and kissing him on the cheek. "I missed you so much, my darling. How did your trip go?"

Prince Everett took her hands from around his neck and stepped back from her. "What's wrong?" she asked.

"You're a beautiful young lady and have a lot to offer any man, but I'm in love with Abigail."

"You just feel that way because you spent a week alone with her. Spend a week with me, and you will feel the same way about me," said Lady Vanessa with panic in her voice.

"I have loved Abigail from the first time we met, and I will always love her. She's the only one for me. I will admit, this weekend confirmed the feelings I've always had. But they're not going to change."

Lady Vanessa reached out and took the prince's hand. "Give it some time. You will see. You will change your mind."

"I'm sorry that you got caught up in all of this, but there will never be anyone for me but her."

Crying, Lady Vanessa began walking to her car. "This isn't over. You will see. I will be a princess," she said under her breath as she got into her car and rode away. Prince Everett felt bad that he had hurt her, but he knew he had done the right thing by ending their relationship.

He went back to his room, pacing back and forth, waiting for Abigail to return. He went over and over in his mind what he was going to say when he saw her. In the early morning hours, he fell asleep in his chair. He hadn't been asleep long when he awoke to the sound of Princess Abigail's door closing. He quickly jumped up and looked into her room from their joining door. He saw her on her knees on the floor, with her face in her hands, weeping. He knew the worst must have happened. Without hesitation, he walked into her room, picked her up in his broad, strong arms, sat down with her on her sofa, and held her firmly while she cried.

Princess Abigail woke up, realizing she had slept the entire night in the prince's arms. She enjoyed the warmth and the comfort of his strong embrace. It felt so natural, as though she belonged there. She looked up at his face, studying his chiseled jawline. She just stared up at him and fought the urge to kiss him. She wondered if the love and affection of one woman would ever be enough for him. With doubt in her heart, she gently pulled herself out of his arms to get ready. She knew she needed to get to the orphanage as soon as possible.

The children had lost one of their own, one from the only family they knew. She dreaded walking into that orphanage, knowing that Ruby wouldn't be there to greet her and that she would never again see her sweet little face. She held her breath to keep from crying. She had to be strong for the other children.

When Princess Abigail came out of the bathroom into her bedroom, Prince Everett was gone. She was putting on earrings and holding her necklace in her hand. Someone knocked on the door. She opened it. It was the prince. "Come in. I wanted to thank you for being there for me last night," said Princess Abigail as she was putting on her shoes in a rush.

He smiled. "Truly it was my pleasure. Where are you off to?"

"I'm going to the orphanage. I know the children are hurting, and I want to be there for them. Could you please help me with this?" She held up the necklace that she had been trying to fasten and was having trouble with. She turned around and backed up to him. He grabbed both ends of the necklace. He fought the desire to reach down and kiss her neck. She smelled so good. As he was fastening it, he leaned in to get closer to her. She could feel his breath on her neck. She wouldn't turn around in fear that she couldn't resist temptation.

There was a knock at the door. "Come in," said Princess Abigail in relief. It was the royal press secretary. He stepped into her room. "Your Highnesses," he said as he bowed. He was elated. "You are the buzz of the day with the way you were there for that little orphan girl last night. It was incredible! The people are raving about you and how you're such a good person. I'm here to get your response for the reporters."

"Just say that I'm not a good person, but I'm a Christian, and I was only doing what I should—"

Valerie Zahn

Prince Everett interrupted her. "Instead say, 'I am a woman of faith.' There are a lot of different faiths in our country, and we wouldn't want to offend anyone."

Princess Abigail glared at the prince and said, "Let them be them, and I will be me. As I was saying, I am a Christian. I am not a good person. I just serve a good God, and because of his goodness to me, I am able and required to show it to others. Now if you two will excuse me, I have somewhere that I really need to be." She quickly walked out of the room.

Prince Everett stood there in deep thought. His entire life had been about performance. He always had to care about what other people thought. If he said this or wore that or did this, what would people think? Abigail didn't care what anyone thought about her. She was just Abigail. She was genuine. She was full of compassion, yet she stayed true to what she believed and her convictions. And the people still loved her for it.

Princess Abigail had had a very emotional day. She sat down on the love seat in her room to remove her shoes. She put her hand on the seat where Prince Everett had sat and held her the night before. She smiled. There was a knock on the door. "Come in," she said.

Prince Everett opened the door and walked in. "You're home late. Are you all right?"

"I am. I stayed until they put the children to bed. This has been very hard for them. I wish I could do more."

"They are very lucky to have you in their lives," said the prince as he walked closer to her.

"I don't feel luck has anything to do with it. I need them far more than they need me. I can't fill the role of a mother, but I'm thankful for the part I get to play." There was an awkward silence.

"I guess I should go and let you get some rest. I'm sure you're tired." Everett wanted to tell her how he felt about her and talk about the amazing week they had just shared together, but he knew this wasn't the time. She was grieving. He would tell her at the coming ball that was in a few days.

"I am quite tired. I wanted to thank you again for last night. It really meant a lot to me," she said while holding back a yawn.

"You have no reason to thank me. After all, it was Friday. I consider it our date." They laughed. Before he left the room, he asked, "Do you mind if I accompany you to the funeral tomorrow?"

Surprised, Princess Abigail responded, with tears in her eyes, "I would really like that."

Before the funeral, Prince Everett and Princess Abigail went to the orphanage together. She was very excited for him to meet the children. As soon as she walked into the building, the children ran to her with excitement and started hugging her. When they saw Prince Everett, they were surprised. They became more solemn and bowed. "Your Highness," they all said.

One of the little girls walked over to the prince and grabbed his hand. "Are you Abigail's husband?"

He looked at the little girl with amusement. "I am," he replied. "It's my favorite title." He looked up at Abigail, and she looked at him.

The little girl continued, "Will you let Abigail live here with us? She said she can't because she's married and has certain duties she has to do. If you say it's all right, then maybe she will live here with us."

Prince Everett laughed. "I would miss Abigail too much if she ever lived anywhere but with me. Can we just keep things as they are, and we share her attention?"

The little girl thought about it for a few seconds. "Only if you come back to visit again."

"It's a deal," said the prince as he held out his hand. The two shook on it.

"She will hold you to your word, you know," joked Princess Abigail.

"I'm good for my word, as you know." She smiled. He reached over, brushed her hair away from her face, and kissed her on her forehead. "I meant what I said—that my favorite tile is being your husband."

Princess Abigail looked away. "We should be going. We want to get to the church before the reporters start bombarding us even more than usual."

After the funeral Princess Abigail was her loving, encouraging, supportive self as she loved the children and few people who had come to the service. Prince Everett watched her, in awe of how much she genuinely cared about people. Just when he felt he couldn't love her any more than he already did, he somehow managed to. He had never met anyone like her. He had met some of the most famous and prestigious people from all over the world, and none of them had impressed him more or made an impression on him like she had. He also thought about how much he had been given in his life in comparison to these little orphaned children. He had never truly stopped to be thankful and grateful. He had taken it all for granted. His entire contribution to the world had been a reputation of good looks, partying, and women. He knew he was here for more, and something had to change. He had to change—but he wasn't quite sure how and where to start.

That night, Prince Everett passed by Princess Abigail's room and noticed the door was cracked open. He opened it up a little more to find her in bed, fast asleep. The moonlight spilled over onto her face. He stood there for the longest time staring at her. She was so beautiful. He thought of how he had given her a palace, a title, and wealth, but it would never be enough. She deserved more than he could ever give her.

Chapter Thirteen

Lillian walked into Princess Abigail's room, beaming. "I'm here to get you changed for the ball."

"You look like you're about to explode with excitement. What's going on with you?"

"Oh, Your Highness, I'm so happy! The prince had a talk with Archie and reprimanded him for dishonoring me. He told him I was a treasure and that the right thing for him to do was to marry me. I can't believe he did that for me, a servant. So Archie apologized to me. We hadn't talked since it happened. He had tried to, but I had avoided him out of embarrassment and shame. So we talked things over, and he asked me to marry him, and I said yes! I'm getting married!" said Lillian as she jumped up and down and squealed with joy.

Princess Abigail hugged her. "I am so happy for you."

"I must admit, I was upset at first that you had told the

prince, but now I'm very grateful you did," replied Lillian as she laid out Abigail's gloves.

Princess Abigail interrupted. "I didn't tell the prince—or anyone, for that matter. I wonder how he found out?" She looked over at her and Prince Everett's adjoining door and smiled. "Now I know. He must have left the door open after he came to see what was happening when he heard you crying."

"It's all right. I'm not upset, Your Highness. Quite the contrary. Please don't be upset with him either."

"I guess from now on, we will need to be mindful if that door is opened." They both laughed.

"Now let's get you ready for the ball!" exclaimed Lillian while holding Princess Abigail's dress.

It was time to walk down to the ball, and the prince hadn't come for her yet, which was very unlike him. She heard coughing coming from his room. She knocked on the door.

"Come in."

She opened the door. Everett was sitting on the end of his bed. "Are you all right?" asked Princess Abigail with concern.

"I'm fine." He quickly stood up and started buttoning his suit.

"You look a little pale. If you don't feel like coming tonight, I'm sure people will understand."

"No, I'm fine, really. You look beautiful, by the way. I hope you can save a few dances for me?" said the prince with a charming smile.

"Well, I will definitely give you the first one. After that you need to forget about me and go mingle."

Prince Everett walked closer to her. "Abigail, I only want to dance with you and only you. Forever." He looked intently into her eyes.

Not knowing what to say, she backed away and began walking toward the door. "Can we discuss this later? We are going to be late."

"Yes, but we really need to talk. We can't keep pretending like nothing happened between us, like we don't have feelings for each other." Princess Abigail didn't say anything as they walked to the great hall.

When they walked in, all the men bowed, and the women curtsied. Prince Everett took Princess Abigail's hand and walked her straight to the dance floor. "You promised me the first dance," Prince Everett joked as he turned his head to cough.

"Are you sure you're feeling well?"

"I'm fine. Please stop worrying about me." They stared into each other's eyes. "The last time we danced together was on the beach. I can't stop thinking about you, Abigail, and our last night together at the cottage. When we kissed it was incredible."

Her heart began racing as the memories flooded into her mind. She felt the same feelings stirring up inside her. For a brief moment, it felt as though they were the only ones in the room. She wanted to kiss him right then and there—that is, until she looked up and saw Lady Vanessa walking in. Prince Everett could instantly see the change in her face. He turned to see what she was looking at. He saw Lady Vanessa and knew right away. "What is she doing here?" asked the prince, confused.

"Well, I would think it would be obvious."

"I ended things with her the day we got back from our trip."

"You did?" said Princess Abigail, surprised.

Just then, Andrew approached them. "May I have this dance?"

"Can we talk about this later?"

"You ask as if I have the choice," said the prince as he walked off the dance floor, frustrated.

Princess Abigail and Andrew began to dance. "I haven't seen or talked to you since the weekend you came to my home. I think Everett is trying to keep you all to himself."

"I have been staying pretty busy," said Princess Abigail.

"Yes, I read in the newspaper how you were there for that little orphan girl—"

Princess Abigail interrupted. "Her name was Ruby, and I deserve no recognition for that. I wish no one even knew about it. Everywhere I go people act like I did some heroic thing. It's not heroic to love on a precious little girl at a time when she needed it most."

"Unfortunately, Abigail, your natural character to love and be there for others isn't so natural for everyone else, which does make you a hero. I'm sorry to have brought it up. I know it's a fresh wound, and I'm sorry to have struck it."

"No, I'm sorry. I shouldn't have taken my frustrations out on you."

"You are welcome to take out your frustrations on me any time. Please feel free to share anything with me. The next time you have free time, I would love to spend some time with you."

She smiled. "I will let you know when it's a good time."

Prince Everett stood from a distance, watching Princess Abigail and Andrew dance together. He fought feelings of jealousy, seeing them dancing and laughing. He was feeling worse as the night went on. He tried to stay off to himself, but women kept talking to him, trying to captivate his attention. His eyes were on Abigail the entire night as she danced and talked to different people. All he could think about was wanting to be all alone with her again.

After dancing with several people, Princess Abigail walked off the dance floor to get a drink. Lady Vanessa cornered her. "If you cared about the prince like you pretend to, then you would just leave and be out of his way. He is very confused by your constant presence in his life. You say you only want friendship, yet you demand a night only for you. He doesn't have a chance to find love with you always being in his face. He needs time away from you to even know what he truly wants," she said vindictively. She didn't even stay to hear Princess Abigail's rebuttal before she walked off.

Prince Everett saw them talking and noted how Abigail's face looked as though someone had punched her in the stomach. He tried to get to her, but he was on the other side of the large room, and people kept stopping him.

Princess Abigail stood there, thinking over everything Lady Vanessa had said. Even though she didn't like Vanessa's execution, what she had said was true. For the prince to have a real chance at love, she needed to be completely out of the picture. She remembered hearing the queen mention at dinner one night a two-month tour coming up in a couple of weeks, and she didn't want to go. Perhaps she could go in her place instead. She spotted the queen, walked over to her, and curtsied. "Your Majesty, may I speak with you for a moment?"

The people the queen had been talking to excused themselves and left them alone to talk. "What do you need, darling? Is everything all right?"

"Yes. Everything is fine, Your Majesty. I just remembered you mentioning at dinner the other night that you had a two-month tour coming up that you were dreading. I was wondering if I could go in your place and do it for you? I could use some time away, and the prince has some business to take care of that doesn't concern me. In fact, I would only be a distraction."

"Are you sure about this? Two months is a long time to be away from home and your husband."

"I am absolutely sure, Your Majesty. I was thinking I would leave tomorrow morning and visit with my grandmother since I shall be gone for a while."

The queen thought it over for a few seconds. "All right,

that sounds wonderful. I will make the arrangements first thing in the morning. Thank you." The queen kissed Princess Abigail on both cheeks. Princess Abigail excused herself to pack.

Andrew saw her leaving and went after her. "Why are you leaving so early? Is everything all right?"

"Everything is fine. I need to go and pack. I just spoke with the queen, and I volunteered to go in her place for a tour. I will be leaving tomorrow."

"How long will you be gone?"

"A little over two months," responded Princess Abigail with a reluctant smile.

"Does Everett know about this?"

"No. I will let him know when I see him later on tonight."

"What brought this on so suddenly?"

She shrugged. "I had a conversation with Lady Vanessa, and she made some good points."

Andrew could see the hurt in her eyes. "You're in love with him, aren't you?"

She didn't answer, but her silence and face said it all. "I really must be going. Please excuse me," she said as she quickly began walking up the stairs.

Prince Everett was feeling terrible. He decided to go back to his room to lie down. He looked for Abigail to excuse himself but couldn't find her anywhere. He saw Andrew and walked over to him. "Do you know where Abigail went?"

"She went back to her room to pack—"

"To pack?" interrupted the prince.

"Yes, she's leaving tomorrow and won't be back for a couple of months."

"What? A couple of months! What brought this on?" he asked frantically.

"She spoke with Lady Vanessa."

He didn't need to hear any more. The prince left as fast as he could to get back to his room. He didn't bother telling anyone. As soon as he got there, he banged on Princess Abigail's door. She opened it. He saw she had been packing. "Why are you doing this?"

"I have to go. Don't you see? You don't even have a chance to find someone if I'm always in the way."

He stepped closer to her. He reached for her hand and put it on his chest. "I don't want anyone but you. You are the only one for me."

"You only feel that way because you basically stopped spending time with your single friends, and I'm the only woman you're around. Give yourself a chance to find someone," she said as she pulled her arm away and continued to pack.

Prince Everett grabbed her shoulders and forced her to stop and look at him.

"You look terrible! You need to lie down," said Princess Abigail with concern.

"Stop changing the subject; I don't feel like fighting with you. What do I have to say? What do I have to do to prove my love for you? Please, Abigail, just give us a chance," pleaded the prince.

"Not until you've had a chance without me."

Frustrated, Prince Everett walked to the door and looked back at Abigail. "Do you know what I think? I think you're scared. I think you're afraid to allow yourself to love again for fear of them dying and leaving you like Luke. And unfortunately neither I nor anyone else can make or keep that promise to you."

With tears in her eyes and out of sheer anger, she responded, "Do you want to know what I think? I think the only reason you want me is because you can have pretty much any woman you choose, married or single, and I am just a forbidden prize and a challenge that you refuse to lose."

The prince stared at her in disbelief. For the first time ever, Princess Abigail saw tears in his eyes, and she was the one who had put them there. "Is that truly what you think of me?"

She could see the pain in his eyes, as if she had pierced his very soul with her words. She wished she could take them back, but it was too late. He shrugged while looking at her. "All I can say to you, Abigail, is that I want you and only you, from now until death do us part." He turned around and went to his room. Feeling horrible, physically and emotionally, he changed his clothes and went to bed.

Trying to keep herself distracted, Princess Abigail kept packing and trying to convince herself that she was doing the right thing. She was determined to leave first thing the next morning. His words kept swirling around in her head. She was so full of different emotions, such as regret and anger. She regretted her words, and even more than that, she regretted going to bed angry; the Bible was very clear on not letting the sun go down on one's anger.

The reason for her anger was because he was right, and she never even realized it. She was afraid to give her heart to anyone again for fear of them leaving her, just like her papa and Luke had. She got down on her knees with tears streaming down her face. "Father, thank you for showing me this area in my life that needs attention. I am afraid, and fear doesn't come from you. It keeps me from experiencing your goodness. Please forgive me, and please help and heal me in this area of my life. I give it to you." She stood up, wiped the tears from her face, and got into bed. While lying in bed, she looked at her luggage by the door. She wondered if she was doing the right thing.

In the middle of the night, Princess Abigail woke up, hearing her name over and over. She sat up in bed. It was Everett, she thought. "Abigail, Abigail, please don't leave. I love you." He kept saying it over and over.

She got out of bed and walked into his room to wake him. She thought he might be having a bad dream. "Everett? Everett?" she whispered." He didn't respond. She grabbed his shoulders to nudge him awake. He wouldn't wake up. She placed her hand on his face; he was burning up with a fever. She ran out of the room, yelling for help.

Three servants came running to her. She started giving out orders. She pointed at one of the servants. "You, fetch some ice and water. You, find clean cloths and aspirin, and you, call the doctor. Please hurry and go quickly!"

She ran back into Prince Everett's room and threw back his covers. She knew she had to get his fever down fast. "Abigail, Abigail, please don't leave me," he kept saying.

"I'm right here. It's all right. Please, Lord, let him be all right. Please don't take someone else that I love," she said as she removed his pajama top.

The servants ran in, bringing the things she had sent them to get. She put the ice into the water and submerged the cloths into the ice water. She wrung out the cloths and began putting them on him. She put one on his forehead, one behind his neck, one under each arm, and one under his knees. She kept cycling them as she would resubmerge the cloths in the ice water and wring them out. She also tried to get him to drink some ice water but was unsuccessful. His body shivered, but he remained unresponsive. She just kept praying and doing everything she knew to do.

When the doctor arrived, he jumped right in and gave the prince some medicine. Princess Abigail assisted the doctor and did everything he told her to do. They were finally able to get his fever down to where it wasn't as dangerous. "My diagnosis would be that this is the Spanish flu. You did an amazing job, Your Highness. You did everything that I would have done. You may have saved his life. We'll just have to watch him and pray and hope for the best. He's still in the danger zone. If you would like to get some rest, go ahead. I will be here to watch him."

"Thank you, Dr. Richards, but I'm not going anywhere until he's better." She pushed a chair beside his bedside and held his hand. She prayed until she fell asleep.

She woke to the bed shaking violently. He was going into convulsions. She jumped up quickly, and so did Dr. Richards. "His fever has come back up!" They began repeating everything they had done before. After thirty minutes or so, the fever subsided again.

Princess Abigail sat back down in the chair and began to sob. She had been there for dozens of dying men and never flinched once. She had sympathy for them and did her best to keep them alive, but this was entirely different. This was the man she loved; she had never told him that she reciprocated his feelings. Remembering their last interaction and the look in his eyes was almost more than she could bear.

Dr. Richards walked over and put his hands on her shoulder to console her. "Let's stay positive, Your Highness. He's still with us, and we are going to do everything we can to make sure he recovers."

She put her hand on the doctor's hand and looked into his eyes. "Thank you, Dr. Richards, for being here."

"I must say, he's a very lucky man to have someone by his side who loves him the way you do."

"Trust me when I say that I'm the lucky one," she said

as she stroked the prince's face with her fingers. "Due to the king and queen not being able to be here because of the prince being so contagious, they wanted me to express their gratitude to you for staying by his side." She smiled and kept her attention on the prince.

The prince got progressively better over the next few days but still hadn't woken up and wasn't responding. Princess Abigail only left his side to get cleaned up. Other than that she ate, drank, and slept by his side. On the third day, she went to get cleaned up. When she returned to Prince Everett's room, Dr. Richards was there, smiling. She quickly walked over to the prince. He was awake and coherent. "Thank you, Lord!" said Abigail with relief.

"I will be back tomorrow to check on you, Your Highness. If you need me before then, don't hesitate to call. I know you're in very good hands."

"Thank you, Dr. Richards, for everything," said Princess Abigail. She sat down in her chair beside his bed, took Everett's hand, and smiled at him.

"The doctor said I most likely would have died if it wasn't for you, Abigail. Thank you," said the prince weakly as he kissed her hand.

"I'm not the one you should be thanking. People die every day under the care of trained medical professionals. Look at Ruby."

"Well, thank you for all that you did. And mostly thank you for being here beside me when I needed you most."

She rubbed his face. "It was my pleasure. But please don't ever do that to me ever again."

He smiled.

"This entire time that you've laid here, all I've wanted to do is to tell you I'm so sorry for what I said. You were right about me, and I was angry that you pointed it out. I have been afraid to love again because of fear. And I..." She hesitated for a second. "I do love you."

Prince Everett's face lit up, even in his weak state. "You don't know how long and how much I've wanted to hear those words from you." He built up the strength to lean over and kiss her. Abigail put her head on his chest. "Now get some rest. I don't want you to overdo it. I will be here when you wake up."

Over the next couple of days, Prince Everett went back to normal, other than being extremely weak. He still lay in bed a lot and needed rest, but he was much better.

The prince was in bed, and Princess Abigail walked into his room to check on him. There were flowers everywhere. There was hardly a place to walk because of the number of them. Princess Abigail started reading some of the cards out loud from some of the flowers. "'Hope you feel better soon, Elizabeth.' 'I'm thinking of you. Love, Rachel.' 'Get well soon, Rebecca.' Do you have any male friends other than Andrew?"

Prince Everett laughed. "I do. It's just that women are more thoughtful than men."

"Let's just say, you know a lot of thoughtful women," said Abigail sarcastically.

"You're not jealous, are you?" asked the prince with a smirk as he pulled her closer to him. "You have no reason to be because I only want you."

She looked down and was silent. "What's wrong?" asked the prince.

"I wanted to let you know that I'm still going on the tour, and I will be leaving in a few minutes. I will be back in two months."

Prince Everett quickly sat up in his bed. "Please, Abigail, don't leave. I know you feel the same way about me as I feel about you. You never left my side through all of this. I need you, Abigail. Please."

"It's because of my feelings for you that I have to give you a chance to make sure you find exactly what you want," said Princess Abigail.

"Are you listening to me? You are who I want! Why do you doubt that?"

"From the beginning, I should have never made it a part of our arrangement for you to have a weekly date with me. I feel that caused you to have an obligation to me that kept you from truly feeling free to find what you were looking for. I need for you to have that chance, completely free from me, for you to know for sure—"

He interrupted. "I do know for sure."

"Please hear me out. I need you to have time where I'm

not always around. Where you have absolutely no obligation to me to truly figure out what and whom you want. When I come back, if it's still me, then we will pick up where we've left off. If not, then God has someone better for you, and at least you will know."

There was a knock on the door. "Come in," said Prince Everett.

It was a servant. He bowed. "Your Highnesses, Lady Vanessa is here to see the prince."

Princess Abigail stood up. "Send her in," she said as she walked to the door.

"Abigail! Abigail! Please, Abigail, don't do this."

"I know you don't understand now, but one day you will." She walked out the door. She heard him scream for her as she walked down the hall. She had tears streaming down her face as she passed Lady Vanessa in the hallway. She knew he didn't understand now, but because of her love for him, she had to give him a fair chance.

Chapter Fourteen

Prince Everett barely got out of bed for four days after Princess Abigail left. Everyone thought it was because he was so weak from the flu. The truth was that the only thing weak about him was his will to keep going without her. When she left, it was like the sunshine was gone, and all that remained was darkness. He was so hurt and angry. How could she do this to him if she truly loved him?

On the fifth day of being in bed, he remembered something Abigail had said to him: "You can't let a person be the source of your happiness. The people God puts in our lives are extensions of His love, but they can't be the source of what truly makes us happy." He knew now just how true that was. What if she came back and wanted to end things? Or what if she just wanted to keep things the way they were, and they only remained friends? He would have to go on.

He decided the first step was getting out of bed. He slowly got up and stretched. He was still very weak. He slowly walked into Princess Abigail's room. He literally felt nauseous from missing her so much. He looked all around her room. He could see her in different locations, remembering special moments and conversations they had shared. He knew the biggest thing he missed about her was the light that shone so brightly from within her. He knew the light was her faith and relationship with Jesus—a light that he could also have and knew he needed now more than ever.

He knelt down beside her bed, as he had seen her do many times. "Dear God, I want the kind of relationship that Abigail shares with you. I know I haven't done my part. Honestly, I've never given you much of my time or attention at all. Starting now I want to change that. You know more than anyone that I love Abigail with all of my heart. I'm so grateful to you that you put her in my life and that it wasn't a coincidence. I know a lot of the things that I love about her come from you. Please guide me and lead me in how to get to know you more. I want to be the man and, someday, the king you want me to be. I give myself to you. In Jesus's name, I pray. Amen."

He stood up from kneeling. He felt a peace come over him, a peace he had never felt before. He knew that no matter what happened between him and Abigail, everything would be all right.

The next morning and every morning after that prayer, he read his Bible in the gardens when the weather would allow in the same place that Princess Abigail had read hers. The following Sunday, and every Sunday after that, he went to church. For the first time in his life, he paid attention to the sermons and tried to apply them to his life. He stopped hanging out as much with his regular friends because they didn't seem to have as much in common anymore. He made a couple of new friends who were like-minded in his newfound faith. Although his heart ached from missing Abigail so much, he actually had true joy and contentment that he had never had before.

One night Prince Everett couldn't sleep. He tossed and turned and kept thinking about Abigail. He was wondering if she was missing him as much as he was missing her. He wondered if she even cared about him at all. After all, she had left him, even after he had asked her not to. Maybe she truly did want him to find someone else so she could be rid of him. He knew that she would be the only woman that he would ever love. He also knew that he would have to produce an heir. He may end up in a loveless marriage after all. He wasn't giving up hope yet. He would never give up on her.

He thought about the children at the orphanage. They were probably missing her as much as he was. Then he remembered the promise he had made to visit them, a promise that he had failed to keep. He thought about his schedule for the next day. His morning was free. He decided to go first thing. He knew he couldn't fill Princess Abigail's shoes, but perhaps he could fill a different role.

The next morning he walked into the orphanage. The staff stopped what they were doing and were shocked to see him. They curtsied. "Your Highness." The director asked, "Can we help you with something?"

"Actually, I was wondering if I could help you all with something. I have a couple of hours to spare, and I was wondering if I could volunteer my services. You probably wouldn't want me to do the same kind of jobs as Abigail, like laundry and dishes. It's not that I think I'm too good to do those jobs; it's just that I think it would take more time teaching me than being helpful to you. Perhaps there's something else."

The director giggled and thought for a second. "Today is our monthly staff meeting. Usually Princess Abigail takes the children outside and plays games. Would you be interested in playing tag and hide-and-go-seek?"

The prince got a huge smile on his face, "That definitely sounds like something I can do."

"Wonderful! The children are finishing up with breakfast. I will send them to you in about ten minutes if you don't mind waiting."

"I don't mind at all," responded the prince as he walked over and sat down on a bench.

After breakfast, the children ran up to him. They were very happy to see him. "Hey, you came back like you promised."

"I did. I'm sorry it has taken me so long. I'm planning to come more often if that's all right with all of you."

"It is," said little Bobby as he held onto Prince Everett's hand.

"Where's Miss Abigail?" asked the children.

"She had to travel for her job as princess, but hopefully she'll be back soon with you."

"We miss her so much," said one of the children.

"So do I, and I know she misses you all as well."

One of the little girls motioned for him to bend down so she could tell him a secret. She whispered, "I think you're the most handsome man I've ever seen," she said as she blushed.

Prince Everett laughed. "Well, thank you. You know I'm married to Princess Abigail. We will keep that our little secret." She smiled, and the prince stood up. "All right, everyone. Are you ready to go play some games outside?"

"Yeah!" the children said with excitement. "Let's go!"

They all went out to the backyard. They played tag and hide-and-seek. They had a wonderful time. When Prince Everett left the orphanage, he had an armful of cards, notes, pictures, and several marriage proposals. He was beaming. He understood why Abigail loved going there so much. He couldn't wait until next week when he could go back again.

Princess Abigail was on the train, watching all the beautiful scenery go by. The trip seemed to be going well. She was getting wonderful feedback about the tour. The papers raved about her. Every day consisted of early mornings and late evenings. Even though she stayed very busy, she still thought about Prince Everett constantly. She kept remembering how he had begged her not to go. She wondered if he and Lady Vanessa had patched things up or if he had found someone else. By the look of his personal flower garden in his room when he was sick, he had a lot of women to choose from.

She missed the children at the orphanage. She wondered how they were doing. She loved them and knew they loved her. She only had three more weeks to go. After the tour was over, she was planning to spend a week visiting with her grandmother. She hadn't been able to go before she left for the tour due to the prince being unwell. It probably wouldn't be long before she would be moving back home.

She wouldn't even consider Andrew's offer. He was a wonderful man, but her heart now belonged to another—that is, if he still wanted her. But even if he didn't, she knew that she would always only love him. And with Andrew and the prince being best friends, it would be too painful to see Prince Everett with someone else. She would have to see them frequently, especially at social events. She knew she couldn't do it. She had started in this agreement with the prince, determined not to marry or to fall in love ever again. She had never expected him to be so wonderful. He had changed her mind and her heart.

She didn't want to admit it to herself, but she had fallen head over heels in love with him. How could she have done this? She was strong and didn't need the affections of any man. Why did love have to be so complicated? She could have stayed and had the love her heart desired. Instead, because of love, she had left. She wanted him to have a chance to find what he was looking for without the distraction of her being in the next room or seeing her multiple times a day, reminding him of a week that was a mere illusion meant to make people fall in love. She knew he felt an obligation to her, part of which was her own fault because she had placed it there. If they were ever going to be together, she needed to know it was genuine.

The train stopped. She collected her things. "Three more weeks." She sighed. "Just three more weeks." As soon as her feet hit the pavement, blinding lights were flashing in all directions as photographers were capturing her every move. She was tired and ready for the tour to be over, but she would do her duty and finish strong. She smiled and waved while the crowd cheered.

The tour was finally over! Abigail's grandmother, met her at the train station. "My darling, I missed you so much. You look tired. Have you lost a few pounds?"

Princess Abigail laughed, "Take a breath, Grandmother. I'm just fine...tired but fine. It's so nice to see you too." Princess Abigail hugged her and kissed her on the cheek.

"We'll get you home, and after you've said hello to all of

the servants, you'll have some time to rest before dinner. The servants are very excited to see you. It's been a long time since you've been home."

That night as Princess Abigail lay in her old bed, she felt confused with her feelings. *I'm in the house I grew up in—even in the same bedroom and my very own bed. This has been my home longer than anywhere. So why doesn't it feel like home anymore?* It didn't make sense to her. Even though she loved being there, and with how much she loved her grandmother and the servants, she felt homesick. She knew it wasn't for the palace or the gardens or for her room there. She longed to see Everett's face, especially the way he looked at her. She missed his touch and the feeling of being in his arms. She missed his smile and his laugh. What if he had moved on? Her stomach dropped. How could she live without him?

She looked over at her Bible on her nightstand and was encouraged. She had faced some tough times in her life. She knew that no matter what, God would help her through it.

The next morning, with reporters following her, she walked through the village. She saw all of her and Luke's old stomping grounds. For the first time since his death, it didn't hurt anymore. They were just fond memories. She walked to Luke's grave. The reporters gave her space as she paid her respects. She had brought a fresh bouquet of flowers. She stood there for a moment. "I know you aren't here. For that I'm grateful because I know where you are. I just have to get this off my chest. I love you, Luke. I always will—because love never dies. But something has happened that I never thought could. I have found love again. I never thought that was possible, but I have. It's so scary to think of taking a chance of losing someone again, but here I am. For all I know, I already have lost him because I kept pushing him away and denying my true feelings. I know you would want me to be happy because you truly loved me. So if the possibility still stands, I'm going to go for it. Until the next time, my love." She kissed her hand and touched the headstone.

When Princess Abigail got back home, she was met by her grandmother at the door. Tears were flowing from her eyes. "Are you all right, Abigail? I know it's very hard every time you visit Luke's grave," said Lady Robinson.

"No, Grandmother, it's not that. I miss Everett so much I can hardly stand it. I must leave first thing in the morning. I didn't leave on the best of terms. I have to get back. I hope you can understand."

Lady Robinson hugged her. "Of course I understand, darling. Love isn't easy. Quite the opposite, actually. Do what you need to do. I will be here whenever you can come again. Or perhaps I will have to visit soon."

"I would love that. Thank you for understanding." She kissed her on the cheek. "I must go and pack," said Abigail with excitement as she quickly ran up the stairs.

Valerie Zahn

Princess Abigail could hardly sleep that night because of her excitement at finally seeing the prince. Then her feelings of excitement quickly changed to worry and dread to see if he had found someone else or not. Either way, she had to find out and face the situation. Tomorrow she would know once and for all.

Chapter Fifteen

Princess Abigail's train had arrived. She didn't tell anyone but the chauffeur and Lillian that she was arriving five days early because she didn't want to draw a crowd. On her way to the palace, she was nervous about getting back and finding out whether the prince had moved on. She asked the chauffeur to stop at the orphanage first. She had missed the children so much and really did want to see them. When she walked in and the staff saw her, they excitedly ran and hugged her. "We've missed you! We're so glad you're back! The children are finishing up with dinner. They will be elated to see you."

"I can't stay long. I haven't been back to the palace yet. I wanted to stop by here first and see the children."

"Now that's love! The children have really been enjoying the prince's weekly visits—"

Princess Abigail interrupted, "The prince has been coming here every week?"

"Oh yes. He's been wonderful with the children. He has in no way replaced you, but he's created his own special spot in their little hearts."

Princess Abigail was thrilled to know that the prince had taken an interest in the children. "I've heard that he's gotten several marriage proposals since you've been gone," said Ms. Arnold with a wink. She was referring to the little girls at the orphanage. Princess Abigail thought she meant actual marriage proposals. She instantly felt sick to her stomach. She had tried to prepare herself for the worst. Apparently she hadn't done such a good job. She shouldn't have come back early, she thought.

When the children finished dinner, beaming with excitement, they ran over and hugged her. "We missed you so much! Please don't ever leave us for that long again," said the children.

"I missed you too. I can only stay a couple of minutes, but I missed you so much and wanted to drop by and see you really quickly before I went back to the palace. I will try to come back in the morning."

"Will you bring Prince Everett?" asked some of the little girls.

"Probably not. He has his own schedule, and I'm not sure what he has planned. He will have to come at a time that is best for him. I love you all." She kissed and hugged each child.

"I'll see you tomorrow," she said while waving and walking out the door.

Prince Everett was getting changed for dinner. He heard noises coming from Abigail's room. He was confused because he wasn't expecting her back for five more days. He walked over and opened their shared door. Lillian was unpacking Princess Abigail's things. "Your Highness," said Lillian as she curtsied.

"Where's Abigail?"

"She's at the orphanage. She wasn't planning to stay long. She should be here soon."

"I thought she wasn't coming back until Saturday. What changed?"

"I believe it was you, Your Highness. She missed you and didn't want to be away from you any longer. She may not admit to that, but it seems very obvious."

Prince Everett's face lit up with pure joy. "Thank you, Lord," he said, looking up. "Can you help me with something really quick?"

"Absolutely, Your Highness."

"Come with me."

When Princess Abigail got back into the car, she asked the chauffeur to drive around a little longer. She wasn't ready to go back to the palace quite yet. She wasn't ready to go back to find the prince with someone else. As much as she would try, she wouldn't be able to mask her feelings any longer. After wasting a lot of the chauffeur's time, she mustered up all the courage she could find and decided to face it. She had no choice. She should just get it over with and start dealing with it.

She wanted to be discreet. She didn't want anyone to know she was there, especially Prince Everett. She took a less-traveled way to her room, and no one noticed her. When she walked into the room, Lillian was unpacking her things and putting them away. The chauffeur had sent word to her that Abigail would be arriving soon so she could attend to her. When she saw Princess Abigail, she ran to her and hugged her. "I've missed you so much, Your Highness. I have so much to tell you." She held up her left hand. "We eloped! I'm married!"

"That's wonderful, Lillian! I'm so happy for you." Princess Abigail hugged her again.

"I apologize for not having your things already put away. I was pulled away for another task."

"That's fine. I'm in no hurry. I'm wondering if I should even unpack."

Lillian kept talking about Archie and their wedding, but Abigail heard very little about it. Her mind was only on Prince

Everett. With everything in her, she wanted to ask about him, but she was afraid as to what she would find out. After some time dancing around the subject, she finally asked, "Has anything changed around here since I've been gone? Is the prince well?"

"Oh yes, Your Highness. Mostly good things. Prince Everett is practically a new man. He's so different...in a good way."

Abigail sighed. *His new love interest must be bringing out the best in him*, she thought. She was trying to convince herself that it was a good thing for her to have left. *God had someone better for the prince, and now he's teaching me to deal with loss once again*, she thought. She sat down on her bed with a sad look on her face as she looked into Prince Everett's room. It was dark, and he wasn't there.

"Are you all right, Your Highness? You seem to be down and distracted; you're not quite yourself."

"I'm not now, but I will be. Thank you for your concern and even noticing."

Lillian looked at the clock. "Can you please come with me, Your Highness? I have something you really must see."

"Can it wait until tomorrow? It's getting rather late, and I'm tired."

"No, you really need to come see it now."

Confused by her persistence, Princess Abigail stood up and said, "All right. Let's go." She followed Lillian. "Why are we going this way when it's dark out?" asked Princess Abigail.

"Please just trust me."

"You must really want me to see this," said Abigail as she kept following Lillian. She noticed that she was walking out into the gardens, and she couldn't figure out why when it was so dark outside. Why not wait until the morning? She thought maybe they had new flowers or a new statue. Then she noticed candles and rose petals that made a path that led farther into the garden.

"I will leave you now, Your Highness. Follow the path." Princess Abigail looked at Lillian with uncertainty. Lillian motioned for her to keep walking, so she slowly followed the path.

In the middle of the garden was a beautiful water fountain, which was Princess Abigail's favorite spot. As she got closer, she saw Everett kneeling in front of the fountain on one knee, smiling. Princess Abigail's heart stopped for a second. She couldn't believe her eyes. She stopped walking; tears poured down her cheeks. She felt like she was in a dream. *This cannot possibly be real*, she thought.

She walked over to him. He took her hand and looked into her blue eyes. "Abigail, from the moment I met you, I knew you were the perfect woman for me. But the truth is, I wasn't the perfect man for you. I was selfish. I was only living for myself and what I thought would make me happy. You showed me what true love really is and the only way to find it. Your faith and your genuineness have shown me what I wanted and needed and have put me on the right path.

"I will forever be grateful to you because you helped lead me to the most important reason for living. I desire to spend the rest of my life with you, but I now understand that you aren't the source of my happiness and joy but only the extension of God's love for me. I know we are legally married, but I'm asking you in the proper way this time. The way you truly deserve. You, Abigail, are the person I want to wake up to every morning and the last face I want to see at night. You are the first person I want to tell my good news to and the only person's arms I want to be in when I'm down and need comfort. I will always be in your corner and will stand with you when no one else will. I couldn't bear living life without you. Will you please make me the happiest man in the world and be my wife?"

Wiping tears from her eyes, she responded, "Nothing would make me happier."

Prince Everett stood. He picked her up and spun her around in his arms and then kissed her. "I've missed you so much," he said as he held her tenderly in his arms. "Please promise me you will never leave me again."

"I promise." They kissed passionately again and then just looked into each other's eyes.

After several minutes of enjoying the prince's embrace, Abigail asked, "So what's the next step?"

The prince pressed his cheek against hers. "I was thinking we could have a little ceremony right here in the garden and renew our vows. It could be the two of us and the minister.

Then we leave immediately after to spend a week at the cottage for our honeymoon."

Princess Abigail was very excited. "That sounds amazing!"

"I'm glad…because you know my track record of planning things for us."

She giggled. He kissed her neck and then her lips. "I will be staying in my old room tonight. There's no way I could control myself If I were that close to you. I want to do things right. The way you deserve. We were committed legally, but this time I want it to be more."

With her arms around his neck, she pulled him in closer. "This is going to be a very, very long two days."

"You're telling me," said the prince as he kissed her gently. Princess Abigail slowly pulled herself out of his arms. "We better stop while we're ahead. I guess this means I will see you on Friday," she said as she slowly started walking away.

"I'll be counting down the minutes." said the prince as he watched her walk toward the palace.

At last it was Friday! Time had never seemed to go by so slowly. Lillian helped Princess Abigail dress for the ceremony. Her white dress was very simple yet elegant, with no veil this time. "I think it's wonderful that you're renewing your vows, Your Highness. You seem so much happier and excited this time around."

"It's because I am. I truly am happy. I barely knew him then. I never thought I would feel this way for anyone other than Luke. God has been so good to me." Abigail couldn't stop smiling.

Lillian stepped back. "You look stunning. I've never seen you more beautiful and so happy. I have your things packed."

"Thank you, Lillian. Thank you so much for everything. I hope you and Archie have a wonderful life together as well." They hugged. "It's time, Your Highness."

Princess Abigail took a deep breath, stood up straight, and walked out toward the gardens. She wanted to take it all in and enjoy every moment. Life had thrown her some really tough times, and she was finally truly happy. As she walked out to the garden, she walked the same path she had a few nights back. When she got to the water fountain, Prince Everett was standing there with the biggest smile on his face. She had never seen anyone as handsome as him. She couldn't believe he was going to be all hers.

He walked over to her and held out his arm for her to grab onto. Together, they walked over to the minister. They gazed into each other's eyes. "You may now say your vows," said the minister.

Everett took her hands and began. "I, Prince Everett, take you, Princess Abigail, as my beloved wife. I promise to wipe your tears when you cry. Hold you when you feel insecure. Protect you from all harm and never stop loving and cherishing you. As long as I live, I will only have eyes for you."

Abigail wiped tears from her eyes and began saying her vows. "I, Princess Abigail, take you, Prince Everett, as my beloved husband. I promise to encourage you when all hope feels lost, to be a pillar you can rely and lean on, to be your biggest fan and your dearest friend for all of my days."

"By the power vested in me, and in the sight of God, I now pronounce you husband and wife! You may now kiss your bride." Prince Everett tenderly pressed her body close to his and kissed her passionately like she had never been kissed before. After a great deal of kissing, they went back to their rooms to collect their things as quickly as they could, and off they went for the most amazing honeymoon ever. They didn't leave the cottage very much the entire week; they had plenty to do to keep them occupied.

Ten months after their honeymoon, they were at the palace. Everett was in his room, pacing the floor back and forth, back and forth. He heard Princess Abigail scream out in overwhelming pain. He felt helpless. He was terrified. What if he lost her? What if she didn't make it through? He remembered what had happened to her mother. Then he heard the sweetest sound he had ever heard: his child was crying. He quickly opened the door and ran into the room.

"Congratulations, Your Highness! You have an heir! It's a boy!"

Tears of joy came into Prince Everett's eyes. He leaned down and kissed Princess Abigail. "You are going to be such an amazing mother. I'm so proud of you. Thank you for making me the happiest man alive."

"Well, you deserve a little credit," said Abigail with a laugh.

Prince Everett and Princess Abigail went on to have three more children. Their children's names were Adrien, after Abigail's papa; John, Edwin, and Michael. Prince Everett and Princess Abigail went to their little cottage on the beach every year. They continued to have their weekly Friday dates, and they never stopped visiting and volunteering at the orphanage. And the best part of this story is…it isn't over yet.

Invitation

I think it's safe to say that you enjoy a good love story. However, the greatest love story ever told starts with the Prince of Heaven, who had everything, needed nothing, yet desired to have a relationship with you. Before you ever knew Him or even cared to know Him, you were on His mind, and you continue to be—to the point that He left perfection, trapped Himself in a mortal physical body, and came to this very imperfect world with nothing. He suffered horrifically by being tortured and dying in your place as the sacrifice for your sin and guilt so that one day you would be able to be with Him in His perfect world when you leave this one—instead of the alternative. He did all of this just for the possibility that one day you might choose to love Him back. It's what His heart truly desires. Whether you are aware of it or not, He constantly pursues a relationship with you.

However, the ultimate decision is up to you. The love He has for you is far greater than anything you have or ever will experience in this world, and the benefits to this precious relationship don't just begin when you die but as soon as you say yes to His invitation to have a relationship with Him. Instead of experiencing fear, despair, and hopelessness, when you accept Jesus as your Savior, you immediately receive peace, joy, and hope. Although we live in a world where bad things happen, He will never leave you or forsake you and will help you through any situation that may come your way. You may ask yourself, "How can I obtain such a treasure?"

First, you need to acknowledge and admit that you are a sinner. Like everyone else, you have sinned and aren't perfect, and you need saving. Second, repent of your sins. Confess your sins to God. Be truly sorry for what you have done that is displeasing to God. Third, believe that Jesus Christ, God's only begotten Son, died for your sins, in your place, for your salvation. Fourth, accept God's free gift of salvation through faith in Jesus Christ and His death at the cross for you. Last, dedicate your life to Jesus. He not only saves you from an eternity in hell when you accept Him as your Savior, but He also intercedes for you at all times to God the Father in order to obtain for you God's power in your life to live for Him.

Here's where you stop living for yourself (an empty life that has only left you feeling unsatisfied and always wanting more) and instead start living a life with purpose. Here is where you stop traveling alone on this path that seems to be wandering nowhere and start traveling with Him by your side with a beautiful destination before you—and, wow, what a journey!

Will you accept His invitation? Will you make this simple choice, a choice to love the One who so loves you, by accepting His Son, Jesus? I can honestly say that accepting Jesus as my

Savior has been the best decision I have ever made. He has seen me through the best and worst of times in my life. From the births of my children to the death of my dad, He has been my Rock. He alone truly gives me hope and joy in a world, and in a time, where it seems there is none. He can do the same for you. Will you let Him? This is truly the greatest love story ever told.

Special Thanks

First, I want to thank God, who has blessed me exceedingly and abundantly above all that I could ask for or think. I am eternally grateful for His pursuit and for never giving up on me. He is my first love and forever will be. Second, I want to thank my wonderful husband, Steven. I love and appreciate you more than I will ever be able to express. Thank you for completely supporting and encouraging me along every step in my writing journey.

I also want to thank my amazing children. You are truly a blessing from the Lord. Thank you for your encouragement. I love you with all my heart. Next, I would like to thank my mother, Judy, and my brother, Craig. This book would not be possible without you. Thank you for being my creative team and backbone. Thank you for always being in my corner and being there for me. I love you dearly.

I also want to thank my dear friend and sister in Christ, Elizabeth Johnson. Thank you for your work and input on the invitation of this book. It's truly the most important part. Last, I would like to thank all my beloved friends who have always loved and encouraged and supported me. I thank God for each of you.

About the Author

Valerie grew up in small southern towns. She was blessed to come from a culture where life revolved around Jesus and family. She always had a vibrant imagination and enjoyed all things media related. As a young adult, she attended Lee University, where she majored in telecommunications. After college, she enjoyed a very successful career working as a video editor. She has worked for both local networks as well as a national entertainment network. During this time, she met and married Steven.

After getting married, she continued working until she was blessed with her first child. After becoming a mother, she found that her heart's desire was to be a stay-at-home mother and wife. Since making that decision, she and Steven have become the proud parents of four biological children and one adopted child, as well as serving as foster parents.

While her first loves will always be God and her family, she has never lost her passion for crafting an engaging story. She hopes to turn her stories into a series that will take her readers on an entertaining journey of romance and spiritual awakening. She hopes her writing will bring both an escape from the world's daily problems and a testimony of God's goodness, love, and grace.